"I need a woman in my bed. And, since my son must be protected, then that woman must therefore be my wife. My proper wife."

"You're disgusting!" Catherine snapped.

"I am a realist," Vito said.

"A realist who is hungry for revenge," she extended deridingly, well aware of his real motive.

"The Italian in me demands it," he freely admitted. "Just think, though," he added softly, "how your very British yen for martyrdom could be given free rein. How you could share my bed and enjoy every minute of what we do there, while pretending to yourself that keeping me happy is the price you ____ pay to keep your son hap___

"And y_____ aim to get ou_____"

"This…_____ with a tug she was aga_____ mouth capturing hers with the ___ of kiss that flung her back into the realms of darkness, where she kept everything to do with this man so carefully hidden.

Michelle Reid

THE ITALIAN'S REVENGE

Passion™

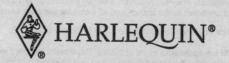

HARLEQUIN®

TORONTO • NEW YORK • LONDON
AMSTERDAM • PARIS • SYDNEY • HAMBURG
STOCKHOLM • ATHENS • TOKYO • MILAN • MADRID
PRAGUE • WARSAW • BUDAPEST • AUCKLAND

ISBN 0-373-12121-0

THE ITALIAN'S REVENGE

First North American Publication 2000.

Copyright © 2000 by Michelle Reid.

CHAPTER ONE

STEPPING out of her son's bedroom, Catherine closed the door just as quietly as she could, then wilted wearily back against it. Santo had gone to sleep at last, but she could still hear the heart-wrenching little sniffles that were shaking his five-year-old frame.

It really could not go on, she decided heavily. The tears and tantrums had been getting worse each time they erupted. And the way she had been burying her head in the sand in the vague hopes that his problem would eventually sort itself out had only managed to exacerbate the situation.

It was time—more than time—that she did something about it, even if the prospect filled her with untold dread.

And if she was going to act, then it had to be now. Luisa was due to catch the early commuter flight out of Naples in the morning, and if she was to be stopped then it must be tonight, before it caused her mother-in-law too much inconvenience.

'Damn,' she breathed as she levered herself away from her son's bedroom door and made her way down the stairs. The mere prospect of putting through such a sensitive call was enough to set the tension singing inside her.

For what did she say? she asked herself as she stepped into the sitting room and quietly closed that door behind her.

The straightforward approach seemed the most logical answer, where she just picked up the phone and told Luisa bluntly that her grandson was refusing to go back to Naples with her tomorrow and why. But that kind of approach did

not take into consideration the fragile sensibilities of the
recipient. Or the backlash of hostility that was going to
rebound on her, most of which would be labelling her the
troublemaker.

She sighed fretfully, caught a glimpse of herself in the
mirror as she did it, then just stood staring at her own
reflection.

Good grief, but she looked a mess, though in truth it
didn't particularly surprise her. The battles with Santo had
been getting worse by the day as this week had drawn to
a close. Now her face was showing the results of too many
emotion-draining tussles and too many restless nights while
she lay awake worrying about them. Her eyes were bruised
and her skin looked so pale that if it hadn't been for the
natural flashes of copper firing up her golden hair then she
would probably resemble some hollow-eyed little ghost.

Not so much of the little, she then mocked herself on an
unexpected burst of rueful humour. For there was nothing
little about her five-feet-eight-inch frame. Slender—yes, she
conceded. Too slender for some people's tastes.

Vito's tastes.

The humour died as suddenly as it had erupted, banished
by the one person who could turn laughter into bitterness
without even having to try.

Vittorio Adriano Lucio Giordani—to give him his full
and impressive title. Man of means. Man of might. Man at
the root of her son's problems.

Once she had loved him; now she hated him. But then
that was surely Vito. Man of dynamic contrasts. Stunning
to look at. Arrogant to a fault. Exquisitely versed in the art
of loving. Deadly to love.

She shuddered, her arms coming up to wrap around her
as if in self-protection as she turned away from that face
in the mirror rather than having to watch it alter from tired

to bitter, which was what it usually did when she let herself think about Vito.

Because not only did she hate him but she hated even thinking about him. He was the skeleton in her past, linked to her present by an invisible thread that went directly from her heart, straight through the heart of their son and then into Vito's heart.

In fact Vito's only saving grace, in Catherine's view, was his open adoration of their five-year-old son. Now it seemed that even that fragile connection was under threat—though Vito didn't know it yet.

'I hate you! And I hate Papà! I don't want to love you any more!'

She winced painfully as the echo of that angrily emotive cry pierced her like a knife in the chest. Santo had meant those words; he had felt them deeply. Too deeply for a confused and vulnerable little boy to have to cope with.

Which brought her rather neatly back to where she had started when she walked into this room, she grimly concluded. Namely, doing something about Santo's distress and anger.

A point that sent her eyes drifting over to where the telephone sat on the small table by the sofa, looking perfectly innocent when in actual fact it was a time bomb set to explode the moment she so much as touched it.

Because she never rang Naples—never. Had not done so once since she had left there three years ago. Any communicating went on via lawyers or by letters sent to and from Santo's grandmother Luisa. So this phone call was so unique it was likely to cause major ructions in the Giordani household. And that was *before* she gave her reason for calling!

Therefore it was with reluctance that she went to sit down beside the telephone table. And with her bare toes curling tensely into the carpet, she gritted her teeth, took a couple of deep breaths, then reached out for the receiver.

By the time she had punched in the required set of digits she was sitting there with her eyes pressed tight shut, half praying that no one would be home.

Coward, she mocked herself.

And why not? she then countered. With their track record it paid to be cowardly around Vito. She just hoped that Luisa would answer. At least with Luisa she could relax some of the tension out of her body and *try* to sound normal before she attempted to break the news to her.

No chance. *'Si?'* a deeply smooth and seductively accented voice suddenly drawled into her ear.

Catherine jumped, her eyes flicking open as instant recognition turned her grey eyes green.

Vito.

Damn, it was Vito. A sudden hot flush went chasing through her. A thick lump formed across her throat. She tried to speak but found she couldn't. Instead her eyes drifted shut again and suddenly she was seeing him as clearly as if he was standing here directly in front of her. Seeing the blackness of his hair, the darkness of his skin, and the long, lean, tightly muscled posture of his supremely arrogant stance.

He was wearing a dinner suit, she saw, because it was Sunday and coming up to dinnertime there in Naples, and the Giordani family always dressed formally for the evening meal on a Sunday. So the suit would be black and the shirt white, with an accompanying black bow tie.

And she could see the disturbing honeyed-gold colour of his eyes, with their long, thick, curling lashes, which could so polarise attention that it was impossible to think of anything else when you let yourself look into them. So she didn't. Instead she moved on to his mouth and let her mind's eye drift across its smooth, firm, sensual contours, knowing exactly what to expect when another telling little shudder hit her system.

For this was the mouth of a born lover. A beautiful mouth, a seductive mouth, a disturbingly expressive mouth that could grin and mock and snarl and kiss like no other mouth, and lie like no other, and hate like no—

'Who is there, please?' his deep voice demanded in terse Italian.

Catherine jumped again, then tensely sat forward, her fingers tightly gripping the telephone receiver as she forced her locked up vocal cords to relax enough to allow her to speak.

'Hello, Vito,' she murmured huskily. 'It's me— Catherine...'

The bomb went off—in the form of a stunning silence. The kind that ate away at her insides and made nerves twitch all over her. Her mouth was dry, her heart having to force blood through valves that had simply stopped working. She felt light-headed but heavy-limbed, and wanted to start crying suddenly—which was so very pathetic that at least the feeling managed to jolt her into attempting to speak again.

But Vito beat her to it. 'What is wrong with my son?' he lashed out, grating English replacing terse Italian. The sheer violence in his tone was enough to warn Catherine that he had instantly jumped to all the wrong conclusions.

'It's all right,' she said quickly. 'Santo isn't ill.'

There was another short, tense, pulsing moment while Vito took time to absorb that assurance. 'Then why do you break your own court order and ring me here?' he demanded coldly.

Grimacing at his right to ask that question, Catherine still had to bite down on her lip to stop herself from replying with something nasty. The break-up of their marriage had not been pleasant, and the hostility between them still ran strong three years on.

Three years ago Vito had been so incensed when she'd left him, taking Santo with her, that he had made the kind of threatening noises which at the time had made her blood run cold with fear.

She had responded by making Santo a ward of court and serving an order on Vito prohibiting him any contact with her unless it was through a third party. Catherine didn't think Vito would ever forgive her for putting him through the indignity of having to swear before a judge that he would neither contact Catherine personally nor attempt to take Santo out of the country, before he was allowed access to his own son.

They had not exchanged a single word between them since.

It had taken him a whole year to win the legal right to have Santo visit him in Italy. Before that it had been up to him to come to London if he wanted to spend time with his son. And even to this day Santo was collected from and returned to Catherine by his grandmother, so that his parents would not come into contact with each other.

In fact the only area where they remained staunchly amicable was where their son's opinion of the other was concerned. Santo had the right to love them both equally, without feeling the pressure of having one parent's dislike of the other to corrupt his view—a point brought home to them both by a stern grandmother, who had found herself flung into the role of referee between them at a time when their mutual hostility had been running at its highest.

So Catherine had grown used to listening smilingly for hours and hours at a time while Santo extolled all his adored *papà's* many virtues, and she presumed that Vito had grown used to hearing the same in reverse.

But that didn't mean the animosity between them had

mellowed any through the ensuing years—only that they both hid it well for Santo's benefit.

'Actually, I was hoping to speak to Luisa,' she explained as coolly and briefly as she could. 'If you would get her for me, Vito, I would appreciate it.'

'And I repeat,' he responded, tight-lipped and incisive. 'What is so wrong that you dare to ring here?'

In other words, he wasn't going to play the game and allow Luisa to stand buffer between them, Catherine made wry note.

'I would prefer to explain to Luisa,' she insisted stubbornly.

She sensed more than heard his teeth snapping together. 'Then of course you may do so,' he smoothly replied. 'When she arrives to collect my son from you in the morning...'

'No, Vito—wait!' she cried out, her long, slender legs launching her to her feet as panic went rampaging through her when she realised he was actually going to put the phone down on her! And suddenly she was trembling all over as she stood there waiting to find out what he would do, while a taut silence began to buzz like static against her eardrum.

The line was not severed.

As Catherine's stress-muddied brain began to take that fact in, she also realised that Vito was not going to say another word until she said something worth him keeping the line open.

'I'm having problems with Santo,' she disclosed on a reluctant rush.

'What kind of problems?'

'The kind I prefer to discuss with Luisa,' she replied. 'Get her advice on w-what to do be-before she arrives here tomorrow...'

No wonder she was stammering, Catherine acknowl-

edged grimly, because that last bit had been an outright lie.
She was hoping to stop Luisa from coming here altogether.
But the coward in her didn't dare to tell that to Vito. Past
experience warned her that he would just go totally ballis-
tic.

'You will hold the line, please,' his cold voice clipped,
'while I transfer this call to another telephone.'

Just like that, he was going to accede to her wishes and
connect her with Luisa? Catherine could hardly believe her
luck, and only just managed to disguise her sigh of relief
as she murmured a polite, 'Thank you.'

Then the line went dead. Some of the tension began
seeping out of her muscles and she sank weakly back down
onto the sofa, her insides still playing havoc at the shock
contact with their worst enemy. But other than that she
congratulated herself. The first words they had spoken to
each other in years had not been that dreadful.

They hadn't torn each other to shreds, at least.

Now she had to get her mind into gear and decide what
she was going to tell Luisa. The truth seemed the most
logical road to take. But the truth had always been such a
sensitive issue between them all that she wasn't sure it was
wise to use it now.

So, what do you say? she asked herself once again.
Blame Santo's distress on something at school? Or on the
dual life he is forced to lead where one parent lives in
London and the other in Naples?

Then there were the two different lifestyles the little boy
had to deal with. The first being where average normality
was stamped into everything, from the neat suburban
London street they lived in, with its rows of neat middle-
class houses, to the neat, normal kind of families that re-
sided in each. While several thousand miles away, in a
different country and most certainly in a different world,
was the other kind of life. One that was about as far away

from normal and average as life could get for most people, never mind a confused little boy. For instead of suburban Naples, Vito lived out in the country. His home was a palace compared to this house, his standard of living steeped in the kind of luxury that would fill most ordinary people with awe.

When Santo visited Naples, his *papà* took time off from his busy job as head of the internationally renowned Giordani Investments to give his son his full attention. And if it wasn't his *papà*, his beloved grandmother was more than ready to pour the same amount of love and attention upon him.

Catherine had no other family. And she worked full time all the time, whether Santo was away or not. He had to accept that he was collected from school by a child-minder and taken home with her to wait until Catherine could collect him.

But all of that—or none of that—was what the child found upsetting. Santo was not really old enough yet to understand just what it was that was disturbing him so much. It had taken several skirmishes and a lot of patience for Catherine to begin to read between the lines of his angry outbursts.

Then, tonight, the final truth had come out, in the shape of a name. A name that had sent icy chills sweeping down her spine when she'd heard it falling from her own child's lips. And not just the name but the way Santo had said it— with pain and anguish.

She knew those emotions, had first-hand experience of what they could do to your belief in yourself, in your sense of self-worth. She also knew that if what Santo had told her was the truth then she didn't blame him for refusing to have anything to do with his Italian family. For hadn't she responded in the same way once herself?

'Right. Talk,' a grim voice commanded.

Catherine blinked, her mind taking a moment to realise what was going on. 'Where's Luisa?' she demanded, beginning to stiffen up all over again at the sound of Vito's voice.

'I do not recall saying I was going to bring my mother to the phone,' he responded coolly. 'Santo is *my* son, I will remind you. If you are having problems with *my* son, then you will discuss those problems with me.'

'He is *our* son,' Catherine corrected—while busily trying to reassess a situation that had promised to be complicated and touchy enough discussing it with Luisa. The very idea of having to say what she did have to say to Vito, of all people, was probably going to be impossible.

'So at last you acknowledge that.'

The barb hit right on its chosen mark and Catherine's lips snapped together in an effort to stop herself from responding to it.

It was no use. The words slipped out of their own volition. 'Try for sarcasm, Vito,' she drawled deridingly. 'It really helps the situation more than I can say.'

A sound caught her attention. Not a sigh, exactly, more a controlled release of air from his lungs, and then she heard the subtle creak of leather that was so familiar to her that she knew instantly which room he was now in.

His father's old study—now Vito's study, since Lucio Giordani had passed away eighteen months after Santo had been born.

And suddenly she was seeing that room as clearly as she had seen Vito himself only minutes before. Seeing its size and its shape and its old-fashioned elegance. The neutral-coloured walls, the richly polished floor, the carefully selected pieces of fine Renaissance furniture—including the desk Vito was sitting behind.

'Are you still there?'

'Yes,' she replied, having to blink her mind back into focus again.

'Then will you please tell me what problems Santino has before I lose my patience?'

This time she managed to control the urge to retaliate to his frankly provoking tone. 'He's been having problems at school.' She decided that was as good a place to start as any. 'It began weeks ago, just after his last visit with you over there.'

'Which in your eyes makes it my fault, I presume?'

'I didn't say that,' she denied, though she knew she was thinking it. 'I was merely attempting to fill you in with what has been happening.'

'Then I apologise,' he said.

Liar, she thought, heaving in a deep breath in an attempt to iron out any hint of accusation from her tone—though that wasn't easy, given the circumstances. 'He's been disruptive in class,' she made herself go on. 'Angry all the time, and insolent.' She didn't add that Santo had been the same with her because that wasn't important and would only confuse the issue. 'After one such skirmish his teacher threatened to bring his parents in to school to speak to them about his behaviour. He responded by informing the teacher that his father lived in Italy and wouldn't come, because he was rich and too important to bother with a nuisance like him.'

Catherine heard Vito's indrawn gasp in response, and knew he had understood the import of what she was trying to tell him here. 'Why would he say something like that, Vito?' she questioned curtly. 'Unless he has been led to believe it is true? He's too young to have come up with a mouthful like that all on his own, so someone has to have said it to him first for him to repeat it.'

'And you think it was me?' he exclaimed, making Catherine sigh in annoyance.

'I don't know who it was!' she snapped. 'Because he isn't telling!' But I can damn well guess, she tagged on silently. 'Now, to cut a long story short,' she concluded, 'he is refusing to go to Naples with Luisa tomorrow. He tells me that you don't really want him there, so why should he bother with you?'

'So you called here tonight to tell my mother not to come and collect him,' he assumed from all of that. 'Great way to deal with the problem, Catherine,' he gritted. 'After all, Santo is only saying exactly what you have been wishing he would say for years now, so you can get me right out of your life!'

'You are out of my life,' she responded. 'Our divorce becomes final at the end of this month.'

'A divorce *you* instigated,' he pointed out. 'Have you considered whether it is that little event that is causing Santo's problems?' he suggested. 'Or maybe there is more to it than that,' he then added tightly, 'and I need to look no further than the other end of this telephone line to discover the one who has been feeding my son lies about me!'

'Are you suggesting that *I* have been telling him that you think he's a nuisance?' she gasped, so affronted by the implication that she shot back to her feet. 'If so, think again, Vito,' she sliced at him furiously. 'Because it isn't me who is planning to remarry as soon as I'm free of you! And it isn't me who is about to undermine our son's position in my life by sticking him with the archetypal step-*mamma* from hell!'

Oh, she hadn't meant to say that! Catherine cursed her own unruly tongue as once again the silence came thundering down all around her.

Yet, even having said it, her body was pumping with the kind of adrenaline that started wars. She was even breathing heavily, her green eyes bright with a bitter antagonism, her mouth stretched back from even white teeth that desperately wanted to bite!

'Who the hell told you that?' Vito rasped, and Catherine had the insane idea that he too was on his feet, and breathing metaphorical fire all over the telephone.

And this—*this* she reminded herself forcefully, is why Vito and I are best having no contact whatsoever! We fire each other up like two volcanoes.

'Is it true?' she countered.

'That is none of your business,' he sliced.

Her flashing eyes narrowed into two threatening slits. 'Watch me make it my business, Vito,' she warned, very seriously. 'I'll put a block on our divorce if I find that it's true and you are planning to give Marietta any power over Santo.'

'You don't have that much authority over my actions any more,' he derided her threat.

'No?' she challenged. 'Then just watch this space,' she said, and grimly cut the connection.

It took ten minutes for the phone to start ringing. Ten long minutes in which Catherine seethed and paced, and wondered how the heck she had allowed the situation to get so out of control. Half of what she had said she hadn't meant to say at all!

On a heavy sigh she tried to calm down a bit before deciding what she should do next. Ring back and apologise? Start the whole darn thing again from the beginning and hope to God that she could keep a leash on her temper?

The chance of that happening was so remote that she even allowed herself to smile at it. Her marriage to Vito had never been anything but volatile. They were both hot-tempered, both stubborn, both passionately defensive of their own egos.

The first time they met it was at a party. Having gone

there with separate partners, they'd ended up leaving together. It had been a case of sheer necessity, she recalled, remembering the way they had only needed to take one look at each other to virtually combust in the ensuing sexual fall-out.

They had become lovers that same night. Within the month she was pregnant. Within the next they were married. Within three years they were sworn enemies. It had all been very wild, very hot and very traumatic from passionate start to bloody finish. Even the final break had come only days after they'd fallen on each other in a fevered attempt to recapture what they had known they were losing.

The sex had been great—the rest a disaster. They had begun rowing within minutes of separating their bodies. He'd stormed off—as usual—and the next day she'd gone into premature labour with their second child and lost their second son while Vito was seeking solace with his mistress.

She would never, ever forgive him for that. She would never forgive the humiliation of having to beg his mistress to send him home because she needed him. But he'd still arrived too late to be of any use to her. By then she had been rushed into hospital and had already lost the baby. To have Vito come to lean over her and murmur all the right phrases—while smelling of that woman's perfume—had been the final degradation.

She had left Italy with Santo just as soon as she was physically able, and Vito would never forgive her for taking his son away from him.

They both had axes to grind with each other. Both felt betrayed, ill-used and deserted. And if it hadn't been for Vito's mother Luisa stepping in to play arbiter, God alone knew where the bitterness would have taken them.

Thanks to Luisa they'd managed to survive three years of relative peace—so long as there was no personal contact between them. Now that peace had been well and truly shattered, and Catherine wished she knew how to stop full-scale war from breaking out.

But she didn't. Not with the same main antagonist still very much on the scene.

When the telephone began to ring again she went perfectly still, her heart stopping beating altogether as she turned to stare at the darned contraption. Her first instinct was to ignore it. For she didn't feel up to another round with Vito just yet. But a second later she was snatching up the receiver when she grew afraid the persistent ring would wake Santo.

'Catherine?' a very familiar voice questioned anxiously. 'My son has insisted that I call you. What in heaven's name is going on, please?'

Luisa. It was Luisa. Catherine wilted like a dying swan onto the sofa. 'Luisa,' she breathed in clear relief. 'I thought you were going to be Vito.'

'Vito has just stormed out of the house in a fury,' his mother informed her. 'After cursing and shouting and telling me that I had to ring you right away. Is something the matter with Santo, Catherine?' she asked worriedly.

'Yes and no,' Catherine replied. Then, on a deep breath, she explained calmly to Luisa, in the kind of words she should have used to Vito, what Santo's problem was—without complicating the issue this time by bringing Vito's present love-life into it.

'No wonder my son was looking so frightened,' Luisa murmured when Catherine had finished. 'I have not seen that dreadful expression on his face in a long time, and I hoped never to see it again.'

'Frightened?' Catherine prompted, frowning because she couldn't imagine the arrogant Vito being afraid of anything.

'Of losing his son again,' his mother enlightened. 'What is the matter Catherine? Did you think Vito would shrug off Santo's concerns as if they did not matter to him?'

'I—no,' she denied, surprised by the sudden injection of bitterness Vito's *mamma* was revealing.

'My son works very hard at forging a strong relationship with Santo in the short blocks of time allocated to him,' her mother-in-law went on. 'And to hear that this is suddenly being undermined must be very frightening for him.'

In three long years Luisa had never sounded anything but gently neutral, and Catherine found it rather disconcerting to realise that Luisa was, in fact, far from being neutral.

'Are you, like Vito, suggesting that it's me who is doing that undermining, Luisa?' she asked, seeing what she'd always thought of as her only ally moving right away from her.

'No.' The older woman instantly denied that. 'Of course not. I may worry for my son, but that does not mean I am blind to the fact that you both love Santo and would rather cut out your tongues than hurt him through each other.'

'Well, thanks for that,' Catherine replied, but her tone was terse, her manner cooling in direct response to Luisa's.

'I am not your enemy, Catherine.' Luisa knew what she was thinking.

'But if push came to shove—' Catherine smiled slightly '—you know which camp to stand in.'

Luisa didn't answer and Catherine didn't expect her to— which was an answer in itself.

'So,' Luisa said more briskly. 'What do you want to do about Santo? Do you want me to delay my journey to London until you have managed to talk him round a little?'

'Oh, no!' Catherine instantly vetoed that, surprising herself by discovering that somewhere during the two fraught telephone conversations she had completely changed her mind. 'You must come, Luisa! He will be so disappointed if you don't come for him! I just didn't want you to walk in on his new rebelliousness cold, so to speak,' she explained. 'And—and there is a big chance he may refuse to leave with you,' she warned, adding anxiously, 'You do understand that I won't make him go with you if he doesn't want to?'

'I am a mother,' Luisa said. 'Of course I understand. So I will come, as arranged, and we will hope that Santo has had a change of heart after sleeping on his decision.'

Some hope of that, Catherine thought as she replaced the receiver. For Luisa was labouring under the misconception that Santo's problems were caused by a sudden and unexplainable loss of confidence in his *papà*—when in actual fact the little boy's reasoning was all too explainable.

And she went by the name of Marietta, Catherine mocked bitterly. Marietta, the long-standing friend of the family. Marietta the highly trusted member of Giordani Investments' board of directors. Marietta the long-standing mistress—the bitch.

She was tall, she was dark, she was inherently Italian. She had grace, she had style, she had unwavering charm. She had beauty and brains and knew how to use both to her own advantage. And, to top it all off, she was shrewd and sly and careful to whom she revealed her true self.

That she had dared to reveal that true self to Santo had, in Catherine's view, been Marietta's first big mistake in her long campaign to get Vito. For she might have managed to make Catherine run away like a silly whimpering coward, but she would not send Santo the same way.

Not even over my dead body, Catherine vowed as she prepared for bed that night...

pleaded. And—well, there is the chance he may refuse to
help, without . . .' She trailed away, saying anxiously, 'You do
understand that I won't allow him to bully me if he doesn't
want to?

'It isn't a problem,' . . . . Then Leo looked at Sa-
Ewell again, as deserved out we 'What! Does that Santo had

CHAPTER TWO

AFTER spending the night tossing and turning, at around
five o'clock the next morning Catherine finally gave up
trying to sleep, and was just dragging herself out of bed
when the distinctive sound of a black cab rumbling to a
halt outside in the street caught her attention. A couple of
her neighbours often commuted by taxi early in the morning if they were having to catch an early train somewhere,
so she didn't think twice about it as she padded off to use
the bathroom.

Anyway, her mind was busy with other things, like the
day ahead of her, which was promising to be as traumatic
as the evening that had preceded it.

On her way past his room, she slid open her son's door
to check if he was still sleeping. The sight of his dark head
peeping out from a snuggle of brightly printed duvet was
reassuring. At least Santo had managed to sleep through his
worries.

Closing the door again, she went downstairs with the
intention of making herself a large pot of coffee over which
she hoped to revive herself before the next round of battles
commenced—but a shadow suddenly distorting the early-
morning daylight seeping in through the frosted glass panel
in her front door made her pause.

Glancing up, she saw the dark bulk of a human body
standing in her porch. Her frown deepened. Surely it was
too early for the postman? she asked herself, yet still continued to stand there expecting her letterbox to open and a
wad of post to come sliding through it. But when instead

of bending the dark figure lifted a hand towards her doorbell, Catherine was suddenly leaping into action.

In her urgency to stop whoever it was from ringing the bell and waking up her son she was pulling the door open without really thinking clearly about what she was doing. So it was only after the door opened wide on the motion that she realised she had gone to bed last night without putting the safety chain on.

By then it didn't matter. It was already too late to remember caution, and all the other safety rules that were a natural part of living these days, when she found herself staring at the very last person she'd expected to see standing on her doorstep.

Her heart took a quivering dive to her stomach, the shock of seeing Vito in the actual flesh for the first time in three long years so debilitating that for the next whole minute she couldn't seem to function on any other level than sight.

A sight that absorbed in one dizzying glance every hard-edged, clean-cut detail, from the cold sting of his eyes to the grim slant of his mouth and even the way he had one side of his jacket shoved casually aside so he could thrust a hand into his trouser pocket—though she wasn't aware of her eyes dipping down that low over him.

He was wearing a black dinner suit and a white shirt that conjured up the picture she had built of him the night before; only the bow tie was missing, and the top button of the shirt yanked impatiently open at his lean brown throat.

Had he come here directly from storming out of his house in Naples? she wondered. And decided he had to have done to get here to London this quickly. But if his haste in getting here was supposed to impress her by how seriously he was taking her concerns about Santo—then it didn't.

She didn't want him here. And, worse, she didn't want to watch those honeyed eyes of his drift over her on a very slow and very comprehensive scan of her person, as if she was still one of his possessions.

And the fact that she became acutely aware of her own sleep-mussed state didn't enamour her, either. He had no right to study the way her tangled mass of copper-gold hair was hanging limp about her shoulders, or the fact that she was standing here in thin white cotton that barely hid what it covered.

Then his gaze moved lower, jet-black lashes sinking over golden eyes that seemed to draw a caressing line across the surface of her skin as they moved over the pair of loose-fitting pyjama shorts which left much of her slender legs on show. And Catherine felt something very old and very basic spring to life inside her.

It was called sexual arousal. The man had always only had to look at her like this to make her make her so aware of herself that she could barely think straight.

'What are you doing here?' she lashed out in sheer re-taliation.

Arrogance personified, she observed, as a black eyebrow arched and those incredible eyes somehow managed to dis-parage her down the length of his roman nose, despite the fact that she stood a deep step higher than him, which placed them almost at a level.

'I would have thought that was obvious,' Vito coolly replied. 'I am here to see my son.'

'It's only five o'clock,' she protested. 'Santo is still asleep.'

'I am well aware of the time, Catherine,' he replied rather heavily, and something passed across his face—a weariness she hadn't noticed was there until that moment.

Which was the point when she began to notice other things about him. He looked older than she would have expected, for instance. The signs of a carefully honed cynicism were scoring grooves into his handsome face where once none had been. And the corners of his firm mouth were turned down slightly, as if he never let himself smile much any more.

Seeing that for some reason made her insides hurt. And the sensation infuriated her because she didn't want to feel anything but total indifference for this man's state of mind.

'How did you get here so quickly, anyway?' she asked with surly shortness.

'I flew myself in overnight,' he replied. 'Then came directly here from the airport.'

Which meant he must have been on the go all night, she concluded. Then another thought sent an icy chill slithering down her spine.

After flying half the night, had he then driven himself here in one of the supercharged death-traps he tended to favour? Glancing over his shoulder, she expected to see some long, low, sleek growling monster of a car crouching by the curbside, but there wasn't one.

Then she remembered hearing a taxi cab pulling up a few minutes earlier and realised with a new kind of shock that Vito must have used it to travel here from the airport.

Now that must have been a novelty for him, she mused, eyeing him curiously. Vito always liked to be in the driver's seat, whether that be behind the controls of his plane or the wheel of a car—or even in his sex-life!

'Which airport did you fly in to?' she asked, the thrifty housekeeper in her wanting to assess the cost of such a long cab journey.

'Does it matter?' He flashed her a look of irritation. 'And do we have to have this conversation here on the doorstep?' he then added tersely, his dark head turning to take in the neat residential street with its rows of neat windows—some of which had curtains twitching curiously because their voices must be carrying on the still morning air.

Vito wasn't a doorstep man, Catherine mused wryly. He was the greatly admired and very respected head of the world-renowned Giordani Investment Bank, cum expert troubleshooter for any ailing business brought under his wing. People valued his opinion and his advice—and welcomed him with open arms when he came to call.

But she was not one of those people, she reminded herself sternly. She owed Vito nothing, and respected him not at all. 'You're not welcome here,' she told him coldly.

'My son may beg to differ,' he returned, responding to her hostile tone with a slight tensing of his jaw.

Much as she would have liked to protest that claim, Catherine knew that she couldn't. 'Then why don't you come back—in a couple of hours', say, when he is sure to be awake?' she suggested, and was about to shut the door in his face when those golden eyes began to flash.

'Shut that door and you will regret it,' he warned very grimly.

To her annoyance, she hesitated, hating herself for being influenced by his tone. And the atmosphere between them thrummed with a mutual antagonism. Neither liked the other; neither attempted to hide it.

'I would have thought it was excruciatingly obvious that you and I need to talk *before* Santo is awake,' he added with rasping derision. 'Why the hell else do you think I have knocked myself out trying to get here this early?'

Once again, he had a point, and Catherine knew she was being petty, but it didn't stop her from standing there like a stone wall protecting her own threshold. Old habits died hard, and refusing to give an inch to Vito in case he took the whole mile from her had become second nature during their long and battle-zoned association.

'*You* called *me*, Catherine,' he then reminded her grimly. 'An unprecedented act in itself. You voiced your concerns to me and I have responded. Now show a little grace,' he suggested, 'and at least acknowledge that my coming here is worthy of some consideration.'

As set-downs went, Catherine supposed that that one was as good as any Vito had ever doled out to her, as she felt herself come withering down from proudly hostile to childishly petty in one fell swoop.

She stepped back without uttering another word and, stiff-faced, eyes lowered, invited her husband of six long years to enter her home for the first time. He did it slowly—stepping over her threshold in a measured way which suggested that he too was aware of the significance of the occasion.

Then suddenly he was there right beside her, sharing the narrow space in her small hallway and filling it with the sheer power of his presence. And Catherine felt the tension build inside her as she stood there and absorbed—literally absorbed—his superior height, his superior breadth, his superior physical strength that had not been so evident while she'd kept him outside, standing nine inches lower and therefore nine inches less the man she should have remembered him to be.

She could smell the unique scent of his skin, feel the vibrations of his body as he paused a mere hair's breadth away from her to send her nerve-ends on a rampage of wild, scattering panic in recognition of how dangerous those vibrations were to them.

Six years ago it had taken one look for them to fall on each other in a fever of sexual craving. Now here they were, several years of bitter enmity on—and yet she could feel the same hunger beginning to wrap itself around her.

Oh, damn, she cursed silently, though whether she was cursing herself for being so weak of the flesh or Vito for being the sexual animal he undoubtedly was, she wasn't quite certain.

'This way,' she mumbled, snaking her way around him so that their bodies did not brush.

She led the way to her sitting room, shrouded still by the curtains drawn across the window. With a jerk she stepped sideways, to allow him to enter, then watched defensively as his eyes moved over his strange surroundings.

Plain blue carpet and curtains, two small linen sofas, a television set, a couple of low tables and a bookcase was all the small room would take comfortably, except for a special corner of the room dedicated to Santo, where his books, games and toys were stacked on and around a low play table.

It was all very neat, very—ordinary. Nothing like the several elegant and spacious reception rooms filled with priceless antiques in Vito's home. Or the huge playroom her son had all to himself, filled with everything a little boy could possibly dream of. A point Catherine was made suddenly acutely aware of when she glimpsed the brief twitch along Vito's jawline as he too made the comparison.

'I'll go and get dressed,' she said, dipping her head to hide her expression as she turned for the door again and—she admitted it—escape, before she was tempted to say something nasty about money not being everything.

But his hand capturing her wrist stopped her. 'I am no snob, Catherine,' he murmured sombrely. 'I know and appreciate how happy and comfortable Santo has been living here with you.'

'Please let go of my wrist,' she said, not interested in receiving his commendation on anything. She was too concerned about the streak of heat that was flowing up her arm from the point where his fingers circled her.

'I am no woman-beater either,' he tagged on very grimly.

'That's very odd,' she countered as he dropped her wrist. 'For I seem to remember that the last time we stood alone in a room you were threatening to do just that to me.'

'Words, Catherine,' he sighed, half turning away from her. 'I was angry, and those words were empty of any real threat to you, as you well know.'

'Do I?' Her smile was wry to say the least. 'We were strangers, Vito. We were strangers then and we are strangers now. I never, ever knew what you were thinking.'

'Except in bed,' he said, swinging back to look at her, the grimness replaced by a deeply mocking cynicism. 'You knew exactly what I was thinking there.'

Catherine tossed her head at him, matching him expression for cynical expression. 'Shame, then, that we couldn't spend twenty-four hours there instead of the odd six,' she said. 'And I really don't want to have this kind of conversation with you,' she added. 'It proves nothing and only clouds the issues of real importance where Santo is concerned.'

'Our relationship—or the lack of it—*is* the important issue for Santo, I would have thought.'

'No.' She denied that. 'The important issue for Santo is the prospect of his father marrying a woman his son is actively afraid of.'

Vito stiffened. 'Define "afraid",' he commanded.

Catherine stared at him. 'Afraid as in frightened—how else would you like me to put it?'

'Of Marietta?' His frown was strong with disbelief. 'He must have misunderstood something she said to him,' he murmured thoughtfully. 'You must know his Italian is not as well-formed as his English.'

Oh, right, Catherine thought. It couldn't *possibly* be Marietta's fault. Not in a Giordani's eyes!

'I'm going to get dressed,' she clipped, abandoning the useless argument by moving back into the hallway.

'Do you mind if I make myself a cup of coffee while you do that?'

Without a word, she diverted towards the kitchen—but,

aware that Vito was following her, Catherine sensed him pause to glance up the stairwell, as if he was hoping his son would suddenly appear.

He didn't—and he wouldn't, she predicted, as she continued on into the kitchen. Santo was by nature a creature of habit. His inner alarm clock was set for seven, so seven o'clock was the time he would awaken.

She was over by the sink filling the kettle with water by the time Vito came in the room. The hairs on the back of her neck began to prickle, picking up on his narrowed scrutiny of her, which once again made her acutely aware of the unsuitability of her present clothing.

Not that she was in any way underdressed, she quickly assured herself. The pair of shorts and a shirt-style top she was wearing were adequate enough—it was the lack of anything beneath them that was making her feel so conscious of those oh, too knowing eyes.

'I don't suppose you expect to hear from him until seven,' he murmured suddenly.

Catherine smiled a wry smile to herself as she transferred the kettle to its base and switched it on. So, his attention was firmly fixed on Santo—which put her well and truly in her place!

'You know his routine, then,' she answered lightly. 'And, knowing it, you must also know that if I try to waken him any earlier—'

'He will not be fit to live with,' Vito finished for her. 'Yes, I am aware of that.'

She glanced up at the kitchen clock, heard a sound of rustling cloth behind her and had an itchy feeling that Vito was also checking the time on his wristwatch.

Five thirty, she noted. That meant they had a whole hour and a half to endure each other's exclusive company. Could they stand it? she wondered, counting coffee scoops into the filter jug.

'Your hair is shorter than I remember.'

Her mind went blank, the next scoopful of coffee freezing on its way to the jug. After only just reassuring herself that he wasn't interested in anything about her personally, it came as a shock to discover that her instincts had indeed been working perfectly.

What else had he noticed? The way her shorts tended to cling to the cleft between her buttocks? Or, worse, that as she stood like this, in profile to him, he could see the shadowy outline of her right breast through the thin white cotton?

'I'm three years older,' she replied, though what that was supposed to mean even she didn't know, because she was too engrossed in a whole host of sensations that were beginning to attack her. All of them to do with sex, and sexual awareness, and this damn man, who had *always* been able to do this to her!

'You don't look it.'

And did he have to sound so grim about that?

'You do,' she countered in outright retaliation.

The rollercoaster of her own thoughts sent the coffee into the jug and saw the scoop abandoned onto the worktop with an angry flick of her slender wrist before she turned almost defiantly to face him, with a flat band of a false smile slapped on her face meant to show a clear disregard for his feelings.

But the smiled instantly died, melted away by the megawatt charge of his physical presence. He looked lean and mean, with his shirt hanging open at his brown throat and his jaw darkened by a five o'clock shadow. He had the arrogant nose of a Roman conqueror, the dark honeyed eyes of a charming sneak thief, and the wickedly sensual mouth of a gigolo. His body was built to fight lions in an arena, but men no longer did that to prove their prowess.

'And memories are made of this...' a silk-smooth voice softly taunted.

Her eyes closed and opened very slowly, bringing her fevered brain swirling back from where it had flown off to, to find him standing there taking malicious pleasure in watching her lose herself in memories of him.

It was like being caught with her hand in the sweetie jar. Sweat suddenly bathed her body, heat flushing her fine white skin—not the heat of arousal but the heat of a humiliation that completely demolished her. She didn't know what to do; she didn't know what to say.

'I'll get dressed...' was the wretched thing she actually came out with, and forced her shaking limbs to propel her towards the door and escape—again.

But Vito was not going to let her get off as lightly as that. Oh, no, not this man, with his lethal brand of wit, who also had so many axes to grind on her exposed rear that he was almost gleeful at being given this heaven-sent opportunity.

'Why bother?' he therefore drawled smoothly. 'It is already way too late to cover up what is happening to you, *mia cara*.'

'I am not your darling!' she snapped out in retaliation, knowing she was only rising to his deliberate baiting but unable to stop herself anyway.

'Maybe not,' he conceded. 'But I think you are wondering what it would be like to relive those moments when you were.'

If she didn't suffocate in her own shame then there really was no justice in the world, because it was what she deserved to do, Catherine derided herself bitterly.

'Not with you,' she denied, with an accompanying little shudder. 'Never with you again.'

'Was that a challenge? For if it was I might just take you up on it. You never know,' he mocked. 'It could be an—interesting exercise to see how many times we can ravish each other in the hour and a half we have free before our son comes down. It would certainly keep our minds off all our other problems...'

If the kitchen door handle had been a gun, she would probably have fired it at him. 'And if you need to sink yourself that low just to keep your mind occupied—then call in Marietta!' She used words to slay him with instead. 'She always was much better trained than me at servicing *all* your requirements.'

So what's really new here? she asked herself as a large hand came to land palm flat against the door to hold it shut, making her blink as it landed. 'You may still possess the body of a siren, Catherine,' Vito bit out, 'but you have developed the mouth of a slut! When are you going to listen to me, you blind bitter fool, and believe me when I tell you that Marietta is *not* and has *never* been my mistress!'

She should have left it there; Catherine knew she should. She should have remained perfectly still, pinned her 'mouth of a slut' shut and ignored his wretched lies until he gave up and let her out of here! But she couldn't. Vito had always been able to bring out the worst in her—and she the worst in him. They'd used to fight like sworn enemies and make love as if nothing could break them apart. It was like meeting like. His Latin fire versus her Celtish spirit. His oversized ego versus her fierce pride.

It had been a recipe for utter disaster. But for the first few blissful months of their relationship it had been a glorious blending of both passionate temperaments fused together by that wonderfully enthralling sensation she'd used to describe as—true love.

It hadn't seemed to matter then that the words were never actually spoken, for they had been there in each look, each touch, in the way neither had seemed able to be apart from the other for more than a few hours without making contact—if only with the intimate pitch of their voices via the telephone. Even when she'd fallen pregnant and the warring had begun, she had still believed that love was the engine which had driven them towards marriage.

Meeting Marietta on her wedding day, and learning that this was the woman Vito would have chosen to marry if she had not instead married his best friend Rocco, had placed the first fragile seeds of doubt in her mind about Vito's true feelings for her.

Yet neither by word nor gesture had Vito revealed any hint that there could be truth in the whispers, and she had very quickly managed to dismiss them when his attention towards her remained sound right through her first troubled pregnancy and into her second.

Then Rocco had been killed in a tragic boating accident, followed within weeks by Vito's father dying from a massive stroke. And before she'd realised quite what was happening, Vito and Marietta had hardly ever been seen apart.

'A shared grief', Vito used to call it. Marietta had called it—inevitable. 'What do you think Vito did when you trapped him into marriage—put on a blindfold and forgot it was me he was in love with? While Rocco was alive he may have been willing to accept second best in you. But with Rocco gone...?'

'I'll believe Marietta's not your mistress when hell freezes over.' Catherine came out of her bitter reverie to answer Vito's question. 'Now get away from me,' she commanded, trying to tug open the door.

But Vito's superior strength held it shut. 'When I am good and ready,' he replied. 'For you started this, so we may as well finish it right here and now, before my son arrives.'

'Finish what?' she cried, spinning to stare at him in angry bewilderment. 'I don't even know what it is we're fighting about!'

'This thing you have against Marietta,' he grimly enlightened her, 'is *your* obsession, Catherine. It always has been. So it therefore follows that it must be *you* who has been filling Santo's head full of this nonsense about Marietta and me.'

Catherine stared at him as if she didn't know him. How a man as intelligent and shrewd as Vito was could be so fatally flawed was a real mystery to her.

'You are the blind one, Vito,' she informed him. 'You are a blind, stubborn and conceited fool who could never see through the charm she lays on you that Marietta is as evil as they come!'

'And you are sick,' he responded, his dark face closing into a mask of distaste as he stepped right away from her. 'You have to be sick, Catherine, to think such things about a person who only wanted to befriend you.'

Befriend me—? 'I'm sorry if this offends you, Vito.' She laughed, almost choking on her own fury. 'But I don't make friends of my husband's lovers!'

Honeyed eyes began to flash dire warnings of murder. 'She has never been my lover!' he repeated furiously.

'And you are such a dreadful liar!' she sliced right back.

'I do not lie!'

'I know Marietta has been feeding her poison to Santo just as she once fed it to me,' she doggedly persisted.

'I will not continue to listen to this,' Vito said, reaching out as if to grab her arm so he could shift her away from the door and leave himself.

'Then will you listen to Santo?' she challenged.

The hand dropped away, his chin lifting stiffly. 'It is what I am here for, is it not?'

Why did his accent always thicken when he was under stress? she found herself wondering. Then blinked the silly question away because it had no bearing on what was happening here.

'But will you believe him?' she wanted to know. 'If *he* tells you that what *I* have been telling you is the truth?'

'And what if it is you who has fed him his version of the truth?' he countered.

Catherine sighed in disgust. 'Which I presume means that you have no intention of believing your own son's word—any more than you once believed mine!'

'I repeat,' he said. 'You are the one with the obsession. Not Santo and not me.'

And I am banging my head against a brick wall here, Catherine decided grimly. But what's new about that? she asked herself, with a deriding twist of her mouth that seemed to set his tense frame literally pulsing.

'Then I think you should leave,' she said, moving away from the door and crossing the room to get right away from him. 'Now, before Santo wakes up and finds you here. Because he will not thank you any more than I do for showing such little faith in his word.'

'I did not say that I disbelieve what Santo is thinking, only that I disbelieve his source.'

'Same thing.' Catherine shrugged that line of argument away. 'And all I can say is that I find it very sad that you can put your feelings for Marietta before your feelings for your son—which makes your journey here such a wasted gesture.'

Vito said nothing, his face locked into a tight, grim mask as he went over to the kettle and began pouring boiling water into the coffee jug. From her new place by kitchen sink Catherine watched him with an emptiness that said she saw no hope for happiness for him. The man was bewitched by the devil. He had to be if he was so prepared to risk the love of his son for the love of that woman.

But was he? Catherine then pondered thoughtfully. For he was *here*, wasn't he? Breaking a court order, willing to risk his visitation rights, because it was more important at present for him to be where his troubled son was. Be of help, if he could. Reassure, if he could…?

'Well, as a tit-for-tat kind of thing,' she murmured slowly, 'let's just test your love for Marietta against your love for your son, Vito.'

'It isn't a competition,' he denounced.

'I am making it one,' she declared. 'And I'm going to do it by giving you a straight choice. So listen to me, Vito, for I am deadly serious. Either you renounce all intention of ever marrying Marietta,' she said, 'or you marry her and forfeit all rights of access to Santino.'

Turning with his coffee cup in hand, he murmured levelly, 'Word of warning, *cara*, You will not come between my son and me again, no matter what tricks you try to pull.'

'Yet pull them I will,' she instantly promised. And the tension between them began to edge up to dangerous levels again, because she wasn't bluffing and Vito knew that she wasn't.

Her father had been an eminent lawyer before his premature demise. He'd had friends in the profession, powerful friends, who specialised in marital conflicts and had been more than willing to come to Catherine's aid three years ago when she had needed their expertise. They'd tied Vito up in legal knots before he'd even known what had hit him.

She would let them do it again if she felt she had to protect Santo from the evil that was threatening to take up permanent residence in his father's house. Vito must be as aware as she was that he had already given her the ammunition to fire at him by breaking a court order to come here like this today.

One phone call and she could make good her threat; he knew that.

'So, what is it to be?' She flashed him the challenge. 'Is it Marietta out of your life—or is it going to be Santo?'

He dared to laugh—albeit ruefully. 'You sound very

tough, Catherine. Very sure of yourself,' he remarked. 'But you seem to have overlooked one small but very important thing in all your clever plotting.'

'What?' she prompted, frowning, because as far as she could tell she had all the aces stacked firmly in her hand.

'Our son's clear insecurity and what you mean to do to ease it,' he said, taking a sip of thick black coffee. 'The last time you went to war against me, Santo was too young to know what was going on. But not any longer. Now he is old enough and alert enough to be aware of everything that takes place between the two of us.'

Pausing to watch as the full weight of his words settled heavily on her, he then gently offered a direct counter-challenge. 'Are *you* willing to risk hurting *his* love for me with yet another one of your vindictive campaigns aimed to make me toe the line…?''

CHAPTER THREE

'NO COME-BACK?' Vito softly prompted when she just stood there, staring at him while the full import of what he was pointing out to her slowly drained all the colour out of her face. 'Am I to assume, then, that your lust for revenge on sins imagined done to you does not run to hurting your son also?'

No, she thought on a chilled little shudder that spoke absolute volumes, she wasn't prepared to risk hurting her son's love for his *papà*.

'Well, that makes a refreshing change,' drawled a man who sounded as if he was beginning to enjoy himself. 'It almost—almost—restores my faith in you as the loyal loving mother of my son *cara*—even if it does nothing for my faith in you as the loyal and loving wife.'

Her chin went up, green eyes suddenly awash with derision. 'If we are going to get onto the subject of loyalty, then you're moving onto very shaky ground, Vito,' she warned him darkly.

'Then of course we will not,' he instantly conceded. 'Let us see instead if we can come up with a more—sensible compromise between us, that will adequately meet both our own requirements *and* fulfil our son's needs in one neat move...'

Was there such a thing? Catherine's eyes showed a blankness that said she couldn't think of one. 'So, don't keep me in suspense,' she snapped. 'Tell me this compromise.'

He smiled an odd smile, not quite wry, not quite cynical. 'I am not sure that you are going to like this,' he murmured.

'So long as it will put Marietta out in the cold, I'll be agreeable to anything,' Catherine assured him recklessly.

He didn't answer immediately, but the way his eyes began to gleam in a kind of unholy way made her flesh turn cold on the absolute certainty that she was about to be led somewhere she had no wish to go.

'Look, either cut to the bottom line of what all this taunting is about or get out of here!' she snapped in sheer nervous agitation.

'The bottom line,' he drawled, dropping his eyes down her body, 'is resting approximately midway down your sensational thighs and has the delicious potential of dropping to your lovely bare feet with a bit of gentle encouragement.'

Glancing down to look where his eyes were looking, she almost suffocated in the sudden wave of heat that went sizzling through her when she realised he was referring to her shorts!

'Will you just stop being so bloody provocative?' she choked, not sure if she was angry with him for saying such an outrageous thing or angry with herself for responding to it!

'I wish I could.' He grimaced, taking a languid sip of his coffee. 'But seeing those exquisite legs so enticingly presented has been driving me crazy since I arrived here.'

It was sheer instinct that made Catherine take a step forward with the intention of responding with a slap to his insufferable face!

But his hand deftly stopped her. 'You still have a great body, Catherine,' he told her, his eyes pinning her eyes with a look that made her feel as if she was drowning. 'All long sensual lines and supple curves that stir up some very exciting memories. So exciting in fact,' he murmured, gently stroking his thumb over the delicate flesh covering her wrist where the pulse-point was fluttering wildly, 'that it occurred to me—long before you showed your attraction to me, I should add—that with you back in my bed I would not need to look elsewhere to fill that particular place in my life.'

A stunning silence followed. One that locked the air inside her throat and closed down her brain in complete rejection of what he was actually suggesting here!

'How dare you?' she breathed in harsh denunciation. 'How dare you make such a filthy suggestion?'

'I need a woman in my bed.' He shrugged with no apology. 'And, since my son must be protected from the seedier side of that need, then that woman must therefore be my wife. My proper wife,' he then succinctly extended. 'One who will proudly grace my table, eagerly grace my bed, and love my son as deeply as I do.'

'And you think Marietta fills all of those requirements?' she scoffed in outright contempt for him.

His golden eyes darkened. 'We are not talking about Marietta now,' he clipped. 'We are talking about you, Catherine. You,' he repeated, putting down his cup so he could free his other hand to slide it around her waist. Her flesh tightened in rejection. He countered its response by pulling her that bit closer to the firmness of his body. 'Who, even dressed as you are, would still manage to grace any man's table with your beauty and your inherent sense of style. And as for the sex,' he murmured in that sinfully sensual tone that helped make him such a dynamic lover. 'Since I know your rich and varied appetite as well as I know my own, I see no problem in our resurrecting what used to be very satisfying interludes for both of us.'

Interludes? He called what she would have described as giving herself body and soul to him *satisfying interludes*? She almost choked on her own outrage, feeling belittled and defiled.

But—maybe that had been his intention! 'You're disgusting!' she snapped.

'I am a realist,' he said.

'A realist who is hungry for revenge,' Catherine extended deridingly, well aware of his real motive.

'The Italian in me demands it,' he freely admitted. 'Just think, though,' he added softly, 'how your very British yen for martyrdom could be given free rein. How you could reside in my home with your head held high and pretend that you are only there because of Santo. How you could even share my bed and enjoy every minute of what we do there while pretending to yourself that keeping me happy is the price you have to pay to keep your son happy.'

'And you?' she asked. 'What do you aim to get out of such a wicked scenario?'

'This…' he murmured, and with a tug she was against him, his mouth capturing hers with the kind of kiss that flung her back too far and too swiftly into the realms of darkness, where she kept everything to do with this man so carefully hidden.

Well, they were not hiding now, she noted painfully as the heat from his kiss ignited flaming torches that lit their escape. And suddenly she was incandescent with feeling. Hot feelings, crazed feelings, feelings that went dancing wildly through her on a rampage of sheer sensual greed.

Only Vito could do it. Only he had ever managed to fire her up this way. Her body knew his body, exalted in its hardness pressing against her. His tongue licked the flames; his hands staked their claim on her by skimming skilfully beneath the hem of her top, then more audaciously beneath the elasticated band of her shorts.

She must have whimpered at the shock sensation of his flesh sliding against her flesh, because his mouth left hers and his eyes burned black triumph down at her.

'And I get my pride back,' he gritted. 'A pride you took from me and wiped the floor with the day you forced me into court to beg for the right to love my own son!'

And without warning she was free.

Standing there swaying dizzily, it took several moments for her to realise just what he had done to her. Then the shock descended, the appalled horror of how easy she had made it for him, followed closely by an all-consuming shame.

And all in the name of pride, revenge and of course passion, she listed grimly.

Her chin came up, her green eyes turning as grey as an arctic ocean now as she opened her mouth to tell him what he could do with his rotten proposition, his lousy sex appeal—and himself! when a sound beyond the closed kitchen door suddenly caught their attention.

It had them both turning towards the door, and freezing as they listened to Santo coming down the stairs, bumping something which sounded rather heavy down behind him. And in perfect unison they both then glanced up at the kitchen clock to note that it was only six-thirty, before they looked back at the door again.

The time was significant. It meant that their son was so disturbed by his worries that they'd woken him early.

From the corner of her eye Catherine saw Vito swallow tensely and his hands clench into fists at his sides. His face was suddenly very pale, his eyes dark, and the way his lips parted slightly in an effort to help his frail breathing brought home to her just how worried he was about what his son's reaction was going to be towards him.

She then suggested to herself an alternative. Afraid? Was Vito's expression the one Luisa had described as his frightened look?

Her heart began to ache for him, despite her not wanting it to. Vito loved his son; she had never doubted that. In a thousand other doubts she had never once doubted his love for his son.

Yet still he didn't deserve the way her hand reached instinctively out to touch his arm in a soothing gesture. And beyond the residue of her anger with him over that kiss she felt tungsten steel flex with tension as the kitchen door flew open, swinging back on its hinges against the wall to reveal their son standing there in the opening.

Dressed in jeans and a sweatshirt, a baseball cap placed firmly on his dark head and his travel hold-all, packed to bursting by the look of it, sitting on the floor beside him, while one little fist had a death grip on the bag's thick strap.

If he'd already been aware that his father was here, then the complete lack of expression on his solemn little face would have been understandable. But he hadn't known; Catherine was sure of it. Their home was old and the walls were thick. And no matter how heated their verbal exchanges had grown on occasion, neither of them had raised their voices enough for the sound to filter out of this room.

So her heart stopped aching for the father to begin aching for the son as Santo completely ignored Vito's presence in the room to level his defiant dark brown eyes on his mother.

'I'm running away,' he announced. 'And you're not to follow.'

It could have been comical. Santo certainly looked and sounded comical standing there like that and making such a fantastic announcement.

But Catherine had never felt less like laughing in her life. For he meant it. He truly meant to run away because he believed that nobody loved him.

And if Marietta had done Catherine the favour of walking in here right now she would have scratched her wicked eyes out.

She went to go to him, needed to go to him and simply hug him to her, wrap him in as much love as she could possibly muster.

Only Vito was there before her—and he was wiser. He didn't so much as attempt to touch the little boy as he hunkered down on his haunches in front of him. Instead, he began talking in a deep and soft husky Italian.

Santo responded by allowing himself brief—very brief— eye to eye contact with his *papà*. 'English,' he commanded. 'I don't speak Italian any more.'

To Vito's deserving credit, he switched languages without hesitation, though the significance of his son's rejection must have pierced him like a knife.

'But where will you go?' he was asking gently. 'Have you money for your trip? Would you like me to lend you some?' he offered when the little boy's eyes flickered in sudden confusion because something as unimportant as money hadn't entered into his thoughts while he had been drawing up his plans to run away.

What was in his bag didn't bear thinking about unless Catherine wanted to weep. But she could hazard a fairly accurate guess at several treasured toys, a couple of his favourite tee shirts and his new trainers, since he didn't have them on. And tucked away hidden at the bottom of the bag would be a piece of tatty cotton that the experts would euphemistically call his comforter, though only she was supposed to know about it and he would rather die than let his *papà* find it.

'I don't want your money.' Vito's son proudly refused the offer.

'Breakfast, then,' Catherine suggested, coming to squat down beside Vito, her eyes the compassionate eyes of a mother who understood exactly what a small boy's priorities would be. 'No one should run away without eating a good breakfast first,' she told him. 'Come and sit down at the table,' she urged, holding out an inviting hand to him, 'and I'll get you some juice and a bowl of that new cereal you like.'

He ignored the hand. Instead his fiercely guarded brown eyes began flicking from one adult face to the other, and a confused frown began to pucker at his brow. Vito uttered a soft curse beneath his breath as understanding hit him. Catherine was a second behind him before she realised what it was that was holding Santo's attention so.

And now the tears really did flood her eyes, because it wasn't Santo's fault that this had to be the first time in his young memory that his parents' two faces had appeared in the same living frame in front of him!

An arm suddenly arrived around her shoulders. Warm and strong, the attached hand gave her arm a warning squeeze. As a razor-sharp tactician, famed for thinking on his feet, Vito had few rivals; she knew that. But the way he had quickly assessed the situation and decided on expanding on the little boy's absorption in their novel togetherness was impressive even to her.

'We don't want you to leave us, son...' As slick as that Vito compounded on the 'togetherness'.

Santos's eyes fixed on Catherine. 'Do you want me to stay?' he asked, so pathetically in need of reassurance that she had to clench her fists to stop herself from reaching out for him.

'Of course I do. I love you.' She stated it simply. She then extended that claim to include Vito. 'We *both* love you.'

But Santo was having none of it. 'Marietta says you don't,' he told his father accusingly. 'Marietta said I was a mistake that just gets in the way.'

'You must have misunderstood her,' Vito said grimly.

The son's eyes flicked into insolence. 'Marietta said that you hate my mummy because she made you have me,' he said. 'She said that's why you live in Naples and I live here in London, out of your way.'

Vito's fingers began to dig into Catherine's shoulder. Did he honestly believe that *she* would feed her own son this kind of poison when anyone with eyes could see that Santo was tearing himself up with it all?

'What Marietta says is not important, Santo,' she inserted firmly. 'It's what Papà says and I say that really matters to you. And we *both* love you very much,' she repeated forcefully. 'Would Papà have gone without his sleep to fly himself here through the night just to come and see you if he didn't love you?'

The remark hit a nerve. Catherine saw the tiny flicker of doubt enter her son's eyes as he turned them on his father. 'Why did you come?' he demanded of Vito outright.

'Because you would not come to me,' Vito answered simply. 'And I miss you when you are not there...'

I miss you when you are not there... For Catherine those few words held such a wealth of love in them that she wanted to weep all over again. Not for Santo this time, but for another little person, one who would always be missed even though he could never be here.

Maybe Vito realised what kind of memory his words had evoked, maybe he was merely responding to the tiny quiver she gave as she tried to contain what was suddenly hurting inside her. But his arm grew heavier across her shoulders and gently he drew her closer to his side.

With no idea what was passing through his mother's heart, Santo too was responding to all of that love placed into his father's statement. The small boy let out a sigh that shook mournfully as it left him, but at last some of the stiffness left his body—though he still wasn't ready to drop his guard. Marietta had hurt him much too deeply for her wicked words to be wiped out by a couple of quick reassurances.

'Where's Nonna?' he asked, clearly deciding it was time to change the subject.

His father refused to let him. 'I promised her I would

bring you back to Naples with me, if I could convince you to come,' Vito said.

'I don't like Naples any more,' Santo responded instantly. 'I don't ever—ever—want to go there again.'

'I am very sorry to hear that, Santo,' Vito responded very gently. 'For your sudden dislike of Naples rather spoils the surprise your *mamma* and I had planned for you.'

'What surprise?' the boy quizzed warily.

Surprise? Catherine was repeating to herself, her head twisting to look at Vito with a question in her eyes, wondering just where he was attempting to lead Santo with this.

'I'm not going to live with you in Naples!' Santo suddenly shouted as his busy mind drew its own conclusions. 'I won't live anywhere where Marietta is going to live!' he stated forcefully.

Vito frowned. 'Marietta does not live in my house,' he pointed out.

'But she will when you marry her! I hate Marietta!'

In response, Vito turned to Catherine with a look meant to turn her to stone. He still thought it was she who had been feeding his son all this poison against his precious Marietta!

I'll make you pay for this! those eyes were promising. And as Catherine's emotions began the see-sawing tilt from pain to bitterness, her green eyes fired back a spitting volley of challenges, all of which were telling him to go ahead and try it—then go to hell for all she cared!

He even understood that. 'Then hell it is,' he hissed in a soft undertone that stopped the threat from reaching their son's ears.

Then he was turning back to Santo, all smooth-faced and impressive puzzlement. 'But how can I marry Marietta when I am married to your *mamma*?' he posed, and watched the small boy's scowl alter to an uncertain frown—then delivered with a silken accuracy the dart aimed to pierce dead centre of his son's vulnerability. 'And your *mamma* and I want to stay married, Santino. We love each other just as much as we love you. We are even going to live in the same house together.'

It was the ultimate *coup de grâce*, delivered with the perfect timing of a master of the art.

And through the burning red mists that flooded her brain cells Catherine watched Vito's head turn so he could send her the kind of smile that turned men into devils. Deny it, if you dare, that smile challenged.

She couldn't. And he knew she couldn't, because already their son's face was lighting up as if someone had just switched his life back on. So she had to squat there, seething but silent, as Vito then pressed a clinging kiss to her frozen lips as still he continued to build relentlessly on the little boy's new store of 'togetherness' images.

Then all she could do was watch, rendered surplus to requirements by his machiavellian intellect, as he turned his attention back to their little witness and proceeded to add the finishing touches with an expertise that was positively lethal.

'Will you come too, Santo?' he murmured invitingly. 'Help us to be a proper family?'

A proper family, Catherine repeated silently. The magic words to any child from a broken home.

'You mean live in the same house—you, me and mummy?' Already Santo's voice was shaky with enchantment.

Vito nodded. 'And Nonna,' he added. 'Because it has to be Naples,' he warned solemnly. 'For it is where I work. I *have* to live there, you understand?'

Understand? The little boy was more than ready to understand anything so long as Vito kept this dream scenario flowing. 'Mummy likes Naples,' he said eagerly. 'I know she does because she likes to listen to all the places we've visited and all the things that we do there.'

'Well, from now on we can do those things together, as a family.' His *papà* smoothly placed yet another perfect image into his son's mental picture book.

At which point Catherine resisted the power of the arm restraining her and got up, deciding that she was most definitely surplus to requirements since the whole situation was out of her control now.

'I'm going to get dressed,' she said. They didn't seem to hear her. And as she stepped around Santo he was already moving towards his darling *papà*. Arms up, eyes shining, he landed in Vito's lap with all the enthusiasm of a well-loved puppy…

'If you still possess a healthy respect for your health, then I advise you to keep your distance,' Catherine warned as Vito's tall, lean figure appeared on the periphery of her vision.

She was in her small but sunny back garden hanging out washing, in the vague hopes that the humdrum chore would help ease some the angst that had built up in her system after having a great morning playing happy families.

Together, they had eaten a delightful breakfast where the plans had flown thick and fast on what to do in Naples during a long hot summer. And she'd smiled and she'd enthused and she'd made suggestions of her own to keep it all absolutely super. Then Santo had taken Vito off to show him his bedroom with all the excitement of a boy who felt as if he was living in seventh heaven.

Now Santo was at his best friend's house, several doors away, where he was excitedly relaying all his wonderful news to a captivated audience, who would no doubt be seeing Santo's change in fortune in the same guise as the child equivalent to winning the lottery.

Which clearly left Vito free to come in search of her, which was, in Catherine's view, him just begging for trouble.

He knew she was angry. He knew she was barely managing to contain the mass of burning emotion which was busily choking up her system at the cavalier way he had decided her life for her.

'Don't you have an electric dryer for those?' he questioned frowningly.

For a man she'd believed had no concept of what a tumble dryer was, the question came as a surprise to her. But as for answering it—she was in no mood to stand here explaining that shoving the clothes into a tumble dryer was no therapy at all for easing what was screaming to escape from her at this moment.

So instead she bent down to pluck one of Santo's tee shirts out of the washing basket, then straightened to peg it to the line, unaware of the way the sunlight played across the top of her neatly tied hair as she moved, picking out the red strands from the gold strands in a fascinating dance of glistening colour.

Nor was she aware of the way the simple straight skirt she was wearing stretched tight across the neat curve of her behind as she bent, or that her tiny white vest top gave tantalising glimpses of her breasts cupped inside her white bra.

But Vito Giordani was certainly aware as he stood there in the shade thrown by the house, leisurely taking it all in.

And a lack of sun didn't detract from his own dark attraction—as Catherine was reluctantly aware. Though you would be hard put to tell when she had actually looked at him long enough to note anything about him.

A sigh whispered from her, and her fingers got busier as a whole new set of feelings began to fizz into life.

'Could you leave that?' Vito asked suddenly. 'We need to talk while we have the chance to do so.'

'I think I've talked myself out today,' Catherine answered satirically.

'You're angry,' he allowed.

'I am?' With a deft flick she sent the rotating line turning, so she could gain access to the next free bit of washing line. 'And here was I thinking I was deliriously ecstatic,' she drawled.

His brows snapped together as her sarcastic tone carried on the crystal-clear morning air. Out there, beyond the low fencing that formed the boundaries between each garden, children's voices could be heard. Any one of them could be Santo, and Vito, it seemed, was very aware of that, because he started walking towards her, closing the gap between them so that their voices wouldn't carry.

'You must see that I really had no alternative but to say what I did,' he said grimly.

'The troubleshooter at work, thinking on his feet and with his mouth.' She nodded, fingers busy with pegs and damp fabric. 'I was very impressed, Vito,' she assured him. 'How could I not be?'

'I would say that you are most unimpressed.' He sighed, stooping to pick up the next piece of washing for her.

Another first, Catherine mused ruefully. Vittorio Giordani helping to hang out washing. For some stupid reason the apparition set her lower abdomen tingling.

'I have a life here, Vito,' she replied, ignoring the sensation. 'I have a job I love doing and commitments I have no wish to renege on.' Carefully, so she didn't have to make contact with his fingers, she took Santo's little school shirt from him.

'With your language and secretarial qualifications you could get a job anywhere.' He dismissed that line of argument. 'Templeton and Lang are not the only legal firm that specialise in European law.'

'You know where I work?' Surprise sent her gaze up to his face. He was smiling wryly—but even that kind of smile was a sexy smile. She looked away again quickly before it got a hold on her.

'Santo has been very vocal about how busy his *mamma's* important job keeps her.'

'You don't approve,' Catherine assumed by his tone.

'Of you working?' Bending again, he selected the next piece of washing. 'I would rather you had been here at home for Santo,' he said, with no apology for his chauvinistic outlook.

'Needs must,' was all she said, not willing to get into that particular argument. They'd had it before, after all, when she'd insisted on continuing to work after they married. Then it had been easy for her, because her multilingual expertise had been well sought after in many fields of modern business. In Naples, for instance, she had managed to pick up a job working for the local Tourist Information Board. Vito had been furious, his manly ego coming out for an airing when he'd wanted to know what the hell people would think of him allowing his pregnant wife to work!

Just another heated row they'd had amongst many rows.

'But the *devil* in this case is definitely not me,' Vito said dryly. 'It is you who refused any financial support when you left me,' he reminded her.

'I can support myself.' Which she always had done, even while she'd been living with Vito in his big house with its flashy cars and its even flashier lifestyle.

She had never been destitute. Her father had seen to that. Having brought her up himself from her birth, he had naturally made adequate provision for the unfortunate chance of his own demise. She owned this little house in middle-class suburbia outright, had no outstanding debts and still had money put away for the rainy days in life. And being reared in a single-parent professional house meant she'd grown up fiercely independent and self-confident. Marrying an arrogant Italian steeped in old-fashioned values had been a test on both qualities from the very start.

But the only time her belief in herself had faltered had been when she was pregnant for a second time and too sick and weakened to fight for anything—and that had included her husband's waning affections.

An old hurt began to ache again, the kind of hurt that suddenly rendered her totally, utterly, helplessly desolate.

'I can't live with you again, Vito,' she said, turning eyes darkened by a deep sadness on him. 'I can't...' she repeated huskily.

The sudden glint of pain in his own eyes told her that he knew exactly what had brought that little outburst on, but where compassion and understanding would have been better, instead anger slashed to life across his lean, dark features.

'Too late,' he clipped. 'The luxury of choice has been denied to you. This is not about what *you* want any more, Catherine,' he stated harshly. 'Or even what I want. It is what our son wants.'

'Our surviving son,' she whispered tragically.

Again the anger pulsed. 'We mourn the dead but we celebrate the living,' he ruthlessly declared. 'I will not allow Santo to pay the price of his brother's tragic ending any longer!'

Or maybe his tactics were the right ones, Catherine conceded as she felt his anger ignite her anger, which sent the pain fleeing. 'You truly believe that's what I've been doing?' she gasped.

His broad shoulders flexed. 'I do not know what motivates you, Catherine,' he growled. 'I never did, and now I have no wish to know. But the future for both of us is now set in stone. Accept it and leave the past where it belongs, because it has outplayed its strength and no longer has any bearing on what we do now.'

With that, he turned away, his black scowl enough to put the sun out.

'Does that include Marietta?' she demanded of his back.

He'd already stopped listening—his attention suddenly fixing on something neither of them had noticed while they'd been so busy arguing. But they certainly noticed now the rows of boundary hedges with varying adult heads peering over the top of them, all of them looking curiously in their direction.

'Oh, damn,' Catherine cursed. At which point, the sound of the telephone ringing inside the house was a diversion she was more than grateful for. Smiling through tingling teeth, she excused herself and went inside, leaving him to be charming to the neighbours, because that was really all he was fit for!

Snatching up the phone from its kitchen wall extension, she almost shot her name down the line.

'Careful, darling, I have delicate eardrums,' a deeply teasing voice protested.

It was like receiving manna from heaven after a fall-out of rats. 'Marcus,' she greeted softly, and leaned back against the kitchen unit with her face softened by its first warm smile of the day. 'What are you doing calling so early in the morning?'

'It's such a beautiful morning, though. So I had this sudden yen to spend it with my favourite person,' he explained, unaware that he had already lost Catherine's attention.

For that was fixed on her kitchen doorway, where Vito was standing utterly frozen, and a hot blast of vengeful pleasure went skating through her when she realised he had overheard her words—and, more importantly, the soft intimacy with which she had spoken them.

'So when I remembered that this was also the day that

your son goes to Italy,' Marcus was saying, 'I thought, Why not drag Catherine out for a leisurely lunch by the river, since she will be free of her usual commitments?'

But 'free' was the very last word that Catherine would use to describe her situation right now. In truth she felt trapped, held prisoner by a pair of gold-shot eyes that were threatening retribution.

CHAPTER FOUR

THE fine hairs all over her body began to prickle as they stood on end in sheer response. 'I'm so sorry, Marcus,' she murmured apologetically, but the way her lungs had ceased to function made every syllable sound soft and breathless and disturbingly sensual. 'But Santo's trip has been—delayed,' she said, for want of a less complicated way of putting it.

'Oh.' He sounded so disappointed.

'Can I call you back?' she requested. 'When I have a clearer idea of when I will be free? Only it isn't—convenient to talk right now...'

'There is someone there,' Marcus realised, the sharp-minded lawyer in him quick to read the subtle intonations in her voice.

'Yes, that's right,' Catherine confirmed with a swift smile.

'Man, woman or child?' he enquired with sardonic humour.

More like frozen beast about to defrost, Catherine thought nervously, but kept that observation to herself. 'Thanks for being so understanding,' she murmured instead. 'I'll—I'll call you,' she promised. 'Just as soon as I can.' And said a hurried farewell before ringing off.

The phone went back on its cradle with the neat precision required of fingers that were trembling badly. 'That was Marcus,' she said, turning a flat-edged smile on Vito meant to hide the flurry of nervous excitement that had taken up residence inside her stomach.

'And?' he prompted, arching an imperious brow at her

57

when she didn't bother to extend on that. 'I presume this—Marcus has a role to play here?'

A role? A strange way of putting it, Catherine mused. Especially when they both knew exactly the *role* Marcus was supposed to be playing. Still...

'That is none of your business,' she told him, provoking him even though she knew it was a dangerous thing to do. But she was too busy enjoying herself, giving him back what he usually gave to her, to care about the consequences.

And body language is such a rotten tale-teller she thought ruefully when she noticed the way she had folded her arms beneath her breasts in a way that could only be described as defiant.

The back door slammed shut, making her jump. A different kind of body language, she noted warily.

'He's your lover,' Vito bit out condemningly.

'But why look so shocked?' she asked, refusing to deny the charge. 'What's the matter, Vito?' she then taunted goadingly. 'Hadn't it occurred to you before that I might well have a personal life beyond Santo?'

A telling little nerve flicked in his jaw. Catherine enjoyed watching it happen. Did he honestly believe that she'd spent the last three years in social seclusion while he hadn't been around to give her life meaning? The man was too arrogant and conceited for his own good sometimes, she decided. It wouldn't hurt him one bit to discover that he wasn't the be-all and end-all of her existence!

'Or is it your colossal ego that's troubling you?' she said, continuing her thought patterns out loud and with derision. 'Because it prefers to think me incapable of being with another man after having known you? Well, I'm sorry to disappoint your precious ego, but I have a healthy sex drive—as you very well know,' she added before he decided to say it. 'And I can be as discreet as you—if not more so, since it's clear by your face that you knew nothing about Marcus, whereas I've had Marietta flung into my face for what feels like for ever!'

'Leave Marietta out of this,' he warned tightly.

'Not while she remains a threat to my son,' she refused.

'The most immediate threat here, Catherine, is to yourself.' He didn't move a single muscle but she was suddenly aware of danger. 'I want this man out of your life as of now!'

'When Marietta is out of your life,' she threw back promptly. 'And not before.'

'When are you going to accept that I cannot dismiss Marietta from my life!' he said angrily. 'Her husband was my best friend! She holds shares in my company! She works alongside me almost as my equal! She is my mother's only godchild!' Grimly, precisely, he counted off all the old excuses that gave Marietta power over them.

So Catherine added to it. 'She sleeps in your bed,' she mimicked him tauntingly. 'She slips poison into your son's food.'

'You are the poisonous one,' he sighed.

'And you, Vito, are the fool.'

He took a step towards her. Catherine's chin came up, green eyes clashing fearlessly with his. And the atmosphere couldn't get any more fraught if someone had wired the room up with high-voltage cable. He looked as if he would like to shake her—and Catherine was angry enough to wish he would just try!

What he actually did try to do was put the brakes on what was bubbling dangerously between them. 'Let's get this discussion back where it should be,' he gritted. 'Which is on the question of your love-life, not mine!'

'My love-life is flourishing very nicely, thank you,' she answered flippantly.

It was the wrong thing to say. Catherine should have seen

the signs—and maybe she had done. Afterwards she couldn't quite say she hadn't deliberately provoked him into action.

Whatever. She suddenly found herself being grabbed by hands that were hell-bent on punishment. 'You hypocrite,' he gritted. 'You have the damned cheek to stand in judgement over my morals when your own are no better!'

'Why should it bother you so much what I do in my private life?' Catherine threw back furiously.

'Because you belong to me!' he barked.

She couldn't believe she was hearing this! 'Which makes you the hypocrite, Vito,' she told him. 'You want me—yet you don't want me,' she mocked him bitterly. 'You like to play around—but can't deal with the idea that I might play around!'

With a push, she put enough space between them to slide sideways and right away from him. But inside she was shaking. Shaking with anger or shaking with something far more basic. She wasn't really sure.

'Until last night—' Was it only last night? She paused to consider. 'We hadn't even exchanged a single word with each other for the past three years! Then you suddenly walk in through my front door this morning and start behaving as if you've never been away from it!' The way the air hissed from her lungs was self-explanatory. 'Well, I've got news for you,' she informed him grimly. 'I have a life all right. A good one and a happy one. Which means I resent the hell out of you coming here and messing with it!'

'Do you think that I am looking forward to having you running riot through *my* life a second time?' he responded. 'But you *are* my wife! Mine!' he repeated. 'And—'

'What a joke!' Catherine interrupted scornfully. 'You only married me because you had to! Now you are taking me back because you have to! Well, hear this,' she announced. 'You may have walked me into a steel trap by saying what you did to Santo. But that doesn't mean I am willing to stay meekly inside it! Anything you can do I can do,' she warned him. 'So if Marietta stays then Marcus stays!'

'In your bed,' he gritted, still fixed, it seemed, on getting her to admit the full truth about her relationship with Marcus.

'In my bed,' she confirmed, thinking, What the hell—why not let him believe that? 'In my arms and in my body,' she tagged on outrageously. 'And so long as my son doesn't know about it, who actually cares, Vito?' she challenged. 'You?' she suggested as she watched his face darken with contempt for her. 'Well, in case you haven't realised it yet, I don't care what you think. The same way that you didn't care about me when you went from my arms to Marietta's arms the day I lost our baby!'

Seven o'clock, and Vito still hadn't come back.

Catherine stood by her bedroom window staring down at the street below and wondered anxiously whether she had finally managed to finish it for them.

She shouldn't have said it, she acknowledged uncomfortably. True though it might have been, those kind of bitter words were best kept hidden within the dark recesses of one's own mind. For it served no useful purpose to drag them all out, and if anything only added more pain where there was already enough pain to be felt.

She knew that he had felt the loss of their second child just as deeply as she had done. And had suffered guilt in knowing that she had known exactly where he had been and with whom he had been when she'd needed him. But in the thrumming silence which had followed her outburst, while she'd stood there sizzling in her own corrosive bitterness, she'd had to watch that tall, dark, proudly arrogant man diminish before her very eyes.

His skin had slowly leached of its colour, his mouth began to shake, and with a sharp jerk of his head he wrenched his eyes from her—but not before she'd seen the look of hell written in them.

'Oh, God, Vito.' On a wave of instant remorse she'd taken a step towards him. 'I'm so…'

'Sorry,' she had been going to say. But he didn't give her the chance to, because he'd just spun on his heel and walked out of the house.

And if the kitchen floor had opened up and swallowed her whole at that moment, she would have welcomed the punishment. For no man deserved to be demolished quite so thoroughly as she had demolished Vito.

Par for the course, she thought wearily now, as she stood there in the window. For when had she and Vito *not* been hell-bent on demolishing each other? They seemed to have been at loggerheads from day one of their marriage—mostly over Marietta. And the final straw had been her miscarriage.

In the ensuing dreadful hours after being rushed into hospital she had almost lost her own life. She'd certainly lost the will to live for several long black months afterwards. She felt she had failed—failed her baby, failed in her marriage and failed as a woman. And the only thing that had kept her going through those months was Santino, and a driven need to wage war on Vito for coming to her hospital bed straight from Marietta's arms.

But that was three years ago, and she had truly believed that she had put all of that anger and bitterness behind her. Now she knew differently, and didn't like herself much for it. Especially when she knew that downstairs in the sitting room, already fed and bathed and in his pyjamas, was their son, kneeling on the windowsill doing exactly the same as his mother was doing. Staring out of the window anxiously waiting for his father's return even though she'd assured him that his *papà* had merely rushed off to keep an appointment in the City and would be back as soon as he was able.

The throaty roar of a powerful engine reached her ears just before she saw the sports car turn the corner and start heading down the street towards them.

And Catherine's hand shot up to cover her mouth as tears of relief, of aching gratitude, set her tense mouth quivering.

From the excited whoop she heard from her son, Santo had heard the sound and recognised it instantly.

Low, long, black and intimidating, Vito's car hadn't even come to a halt when she heard the front door open then saw her son racing down the path towards him. As he climbed out on the roadside, Vito's face broke into a slashing grin as he watched his son scramble up and over the gate without bothering to open it.

He must have gone back to his London home as he had changed his clothes, she noticed. The creased suit and shirt swapped for crease-free and stylishly casual black linen trousers and a dark red shirt that moulded the muscular structure of his torso. And his face was clean shaven, the roguish look wiped away so only the smooth, dark, sleek Italian man of means was visible.

Coming around the long bonnet of the car, Vito only had time to open his arms as his son leapt into them. Leaning back against the passenger door of the car, he then proceeded to listen as Santo rattled on to him in a jumble of words that probably didn't make much sense he was so excited. But that didn't matter.

What Santo was really saying was all too clear enough. I've got my *papà* back. I'm happy!

Glancing up, Vito saw her standing there watching them, and his eyes froze in that instant. Take this away from me if you dare, he seemed to be challenging.

But Catherine didn't dare—she didn't even *want* to dare.

Turning away from the window, she left them to it and went to sink weakly down on her bed while she tried to decide where they went from here.

To Naples, of course, a dryly mocking voice inside her head informed her. Where you will toe the line that Vito will draw for you.

And why will you do that? she asked herself starkly.

Because when you brutally demolished him today, what you actually did was demolish your will to fight him.

Getting wearily to her feet, she grimly braced herself, ready to go down and face Vito. She found them in the sitting room and paused on the threshold to witness the easy intimacy with which Santo sat on Vito's lap with his latest reading book open. Between them they were reading it in English then translating into Italian in a way that told Catherine that they did this a lot back in Naples.

And still she didn't know what her place was going to be in this new order of things. But when Vito glanced up at her and she saw the residue of pallor that told her he still had not recovered from all of that ugliness earlier, she knew one thing for an absolute certainty as shame went riddling through her.

Vito might be feeling the weight of his own guilt but he would never forgive her for making him remember it.

'I'm sorry,' she murmured, because it had to be said now or never, even if their son was there to hear it. 'I didn't mean to—'

'Santo and I are going to spend the day out tomorrow,' Vito coolly cut in. 'To give you chance to close up your life here. We fly back to Naples the day after...'

'Damn...' Catherine muttered as she lost the end to the roll of sticky tape—again. 'Damn, damn, blasted damn...'

With an elbow trying to keep the cardboard box lid shut,

she used a fingernail to pick carefully at the tape while her teeth literally tingled with frustration.

She'd had a lousy day and this stupid sticky tape was just about finishing it. First of all she'd had a row with Santo just before he'd gone off with his father and she'd walked into his bedroom to find it in complete upheaval.

'Santino—get up here and clean this mess up!' she'd yelled at him down the stairwell.

He'd come, but reluctantly. 'Can't you do it, this once?' he'd asked her sulkily. 'Papà is ready to go now!'

'No, I cannot,' she refused. 'And Papà can wait.'

'I never have to do this in Naples,' her son muttered complainingly as he slouched passed her.

In the mood she was in, mentioning Naples was the equivalent of waving a red flag at a bull.

'Well, in this house we clean up after ourselves, and *before* we get treats out!' Catherine fired back. 'And guess what, sweetie?' she added for good measure. 'From now on Mummy is going to be in Naples to make sure you don't get away with such disgraceful behaviour!'

'Maybe you should stay here, then,' the little terror responded.

'Santino!'

Catherine hadn't realised that Vito called his son Santino, as she did, when the boy was in trouble. And it had a funny little effect on her to hear him doing it this morning.

'Apologise to your mother and do as she tells you!'

The apology was instant. And Catherine sighed, and seethed, and resented the hell out of Vito for getting from her son what she had been about to get from him herself.

But then that was just another little thing about herself she'd learned that she didn't like. She was jealous of Santo's close relationship with his father. It had shown its ugly green head when Santo had insisted Vito take him to bed last night, leaving her feeling pathetically rejected.

And the pendulum had swung back the other way, just like that, putting her right on the attack again. So when Vito had come down half an hour later and coolly informed her that their son was expecting him to stay the night—she exploded.

'You've got your own house only two miles up the road. Use it!' she'd exclaimed. 'I don't want you staying here.'

'I didn't say that *I* wanted to stay,' he'd drawled. 'Only that our son expects it.'

'Well, I expect you to leave,' she'd countered. 'Now, if possible. I've got things to do and you—'

'Or people to see?' he'd silkily suggested. 'Like your lover, for instance?'

So, they were back to that already, she'd noted angrily, realising that neither seemed to have learned much from their row that morning. 'I do not bring my lovers into this house,' she'd informed him haughtily. 'Behaviour like that might be acceptable in Italy but it certainly isn't here!'

As a poke at Marietta without actually saying her name, it had certainly hit its mark. His hard face had shut down completely. 'Then where do you meet him? In a motel under assumed names?'

'Better that than allocating him the room next to my room,' she'd said.

The remark had sent his eyes black. 'Marietta never occupied a room within ten of ours, Catherine,' he'd censured harshly.

But at least he had voiced whom it was they were talking about. 'Well, rest assured she won't be occupying *any* room when I move back in,' she'd informed him. 'And if I see her with so much as a toothbrush in her hand, I'll chuck her through the nearest window.'

To her annoyance he'd laughed. 'Now that I would like to see,' he'd murmured. 'After all, Marietta stands a good two inches taller than you and there is a little bit more of her—in every way.'

'Well, you should know,' she'd drawled, in a tone that had wiped that grin right off his face!

He'd left soon after that, stiffly promising to return before Santo woke up the next morning. He'd left soon after her argument with Santo this morning too, she recalled now, with a grimace. One glance at her face as she'd walked down the stairs must have told him she was gunning for yet another round with him.

Next she'd had to beg an immediate release from her contract, which Robert Lang had not taken kindly. Then she'd had to say her goodbyes to people she had been working with for over two years, and that had been pretty wretched. Then—surprise, surprise—something nice had happened! One of the new recruits at the company had come to search her out because he'd heard she was leaving London and wanted to know if he could lease her house from her.

Why not? she'd thought. It was better than leaving it unlived in, and she liked the idea of him and his small family looking after the place for her.

But she hadn't bargained on the extra work it would entail to leave the house fit for strangers. Instead of just doing the usual preparations, then shutting the front door on everything as she left it, she'd had to go hunting round for anything and everything of a personal nature and box it up ready to go into storage, arrange for that darned storage, and also arrange for a company of professional cleaners to come in and get the place ready for her new tenants.

Now she was tired and fed-up and harassed, and all she wanted to do was sit down and have a good weep because everything she'd grown to rely on for security in her life had been effectively dismantled today!

But she couldn't weep because Vito and her son were

due back at any minute, and she would rather die than let Vito catch her weeping!

But none of that—or even all of that put together—compared with the awful lunch she had endured with Marcus Templeton.

Okay, she reasoned, so their relationship was not quite on the footing that she had led Vito to believe. But it had been getting there—slowly. And she liked Marcus—she really did! He was the first man she had allowed to get close to her after the disastrous time she'd had with Vito.

He was good and kind and treated her as an intellectual equal rather than a potential lover. And she liked what they'd had together. It was so much calmer and more mature than the relationship she'd had with Vito.

No fire. No passion to fog up reality.

Marcus was tall, he was dark—though not the romantically uncompromising dark that was Vito's main weapon of destruction. And he was very good-looking—in a purely British kind of way.

She'd wanted to want him. She'd wanted to stop comparing every other man she met with Vito and actually take a chance on Marcus being the one to help her remove Vito's brand of hot possession from her soul for ever. But had she been in love with Marcus? She asked herself. And the answer came back in the form of a dark shadow. For, no, she had not fallen in love with him nor even been close to falling, she realised now.

But what really hurt, what really shocked and shamed and appalled her, was that she hadn't realised just how seriously Marcus had fallen in love with her—until she'd broken her news to him today.

With a heavy sigh she sat back against the wall behind her, her packing forgotten for the moment while she let herself dwell on the biggest crime of blindness she had ever been guilty of.

She had stunned Marcus with her announcement that she was going back to Naples and to her husband. She had knocked the stuffing right out of him. So much so, in fact, that he hadn't moved, hadn't breathed, hadn't done anything for the space of thirty long wretched seconds but stare blankly into space.

The threatened tears arrived. Catherine felt them trickle down her dusty cheeks but didn't bother to stop them.

Because Marcus loved her—and she'd always wanted to be loved like that—for herself and not just the heat of her passion!

Oh, he'd pulled himself together eventually, she recalled with bittersweet misery. Then he'd said all the nice, kind gentlemanly things aimed to make her feel better when really it should have been the other way around and her consoling him.

But how do you console someone you know you've hurt more than you would ever want to be hurt yourself?

'Mummy?' The concerned sound of her son's voice reached deep inside to where she'd sunk in, and brought her shuddering back to a sense of where she was. She opened her eyes to find him squatting beside her with a gentle hand resting on her shoulder and his brown eyes looking terribly anxious. 'What's the matter?' he asked worriedly.

'Oh,' she choked, hurriedly pulling herself together. 'Nothing,' she said huskily. 'Just some dust in my eye. How...?' She rubbed at the offending evidence. 'How did you get in?' she asked.

'The front door was open,' another deeper and very protracted voice grimly informed her.

Vito. Her heart sank. And now she felt thoroughly stupid.

'You left it on the latch.' Her small son took up the censure. 'And we couldn't find you anywhere so we thought something might have happened to you.'

Couldn't find her? Why, where was she? she asked herself with a blank stare at her immediate surroundings.

She was in her bedroom, she realised. Sitting on the floor between the chest of drawers and the wardrobe while the space around her was piled with hastily filled cardboard boxes.

Boxes in which to pack her life away, she thought tragically. And without any warning the floodgates swung wide open. It was terrible—the lowest moment of her whole rotten day, in fact.

So the tears flowed in abundance and she couldn't stop them, and beside her Santo began crying too. He tried to hug her and she tried to comfort him by hugging him back and mumbling silly words about his mother being silly, and somewhere in the background she could hear things being shifted and someone cursing, but didn't even remember who that someone was until her son was plucked away from her and put somewhere so a pair of strong arms could reach down and gather her up.

She simply curled up against a big, firm male body and continued weeping into its shoulder. Oh, she knew it was Vito, but to admit that to herself meant fighting him again, and she didn't want to fight right now. She wanted to cry and be weak and pathetic and vulnerable. She wanted to be held and clucked over and made to feel safe.

He sat down on the bed with her cradled against him and beside them Santo came to put his arms back around her; he was still sobbing.

'Santino, *caro*,' Vito was murmuring with husky firmness. 'Please stop that crying. Your *mamma* is merely sad at having to leave here, that is all. Females do this; you must learn to expect it.'

The voice of experience, Catherine mocked within her own little nightmare. Yet she'd never cried on him like this—ever. So where had he acquired that experience?

'I hate you,' she whispered thickly.

'No, you don't. Your *mamma* did not mean that, Santo,' Vito coolly informed his son. 'She merely hates having to leave this house, that is all.'

In other words, Remember who is listening.

'We'll have to stay here, then,' his young son wailed, his arms tightening protectively around Catherine.

'We will not.' His father vetoed that suggestion. 'Your *mamma* loves Naples too; she is just determined to forget that for now.' The man had no heart, Catherine decided miserably. 'Now be of use,' he instructed his son sternly, 'and go and get your mother a glass of water from the kitchen.'

The sheer importance of the task diverted Santo enough to stop his tears and send him scrambling quickly from the bed.

'Now, try to control yourself before he comes back.' Vito turned his grimness onto Catherine next. 'You are frightening him with all of this.'

She didn't need telling twice to realise that Vito was only being truthful and she had frightened Santo by breaking down. So she made a concerted effort to stem the tears, then pulled herself free of his arms and crawled off his lap and beneath the duvet without uttering a single word.

What could she say, after all? she pondered bleakly. I'm crying because I hurt the man I wanted to replace you with? Vito would really love to know that!

By the time Santo came back, carefully carrying the glass of water in front of him, her tears had been reduced to the occasional sniffle. Smiling him a watery smile, she accepted his offering and added a nasal-sounding thank you that didn't alter his solemn stare.'

I don't like to see you upset, Mummy,' he confessed.

'I'm sorry, darling,' she apologised gently, and pressed a reassuring kiss to his cheek. 'I promise I won't do it again.'

And to think, she slayed herself guiltily, only this morning she had been shouting at him, and here he was being so excruciatingly nice to her! It was enough to make her want to start crying all over again.

Maybe Vito saw it coming, because as quick as a flash he was ushering Santo out of the room with murmured phrases about Catherine needing to rest now.

Oddly enough she did rest. Lying there, huddled beneath the duvet, she started out by thinking about Marcus and Santo and herself and ended up falling asleep, to dream about Vito coming back into the bedroom, she didn't how much later, and silently but gently undressing her before slipping the duvet back over her boneless figure. She could remember dreaming that she had a one-sided conversation with him, but before she could remember what that conversation was about sleep claimed her yet again.

The next time she awoke she knew it was the middle of the night simply by the hushed silence beyond the closed curtains. She lay there for a while, feeling relaxed and comfortable—until something moved in the bed beside her that had her shimmying over on a gasp of alarm.

She found Vito asleep in the bed beside her. Lying flat on his back, with an arm thrown in relaxed abandon on the pillow behind his head, he looked as if he had been there for hours!

But that wasn't all—not by a long shot. Because from what she could see of his bronze muscled torso, he had also climbed into her bed naked!

CHAPTER FIVE

'VITO!' she cried in whispering protest, and issued an angry push to his warm satin shoulder.

'Hmm?' he mumbled, black-lashed eyelids flickering upwards to reveal slumberous eyes that were not quite in focus.

'What do you think you are doing here?' Catherine demanded.

'Sleeping,' he murmured, and lowered his eyelids again. 'I suggest that you do the same thing.'

'But I don't want you in my bed!'

'Tough,' he replied. 'Because I am staying. You could not be left alone here in the state you were in, and Santo needed the reassurance of my presence. So be wise, *cara*,' he advised. 'Accept a situation you brought upon yourself. Shut up and go to sleep before I awaken properly and begin thinking of other things we can do to use up what is left of the night.'

'Well, of all the—' She couldn't believe she was hearing this. 'What makes you think that all of that gives you the right to climb into bed with me?'

'Arrogance,' he replied, so blandly that Catherine almost choked on the sudden urge to laugh!

Only this was no laughing matter. 'Just get out of here,' she hissed, giving his rock-solid shoulder yet another prompting push.

'If I open my eyes, Catherine, you will intensely regret it,' he warned very grimly.

She was no fool; she recognised that tone. On an angry

flurry of naked flesh, she flung herself onto her back, to lie seething in silence.

Naked. Her heart stopped beating as a new kind of shock went rampaging through her.

So it had not been a dream and Vito *had* undressed her! The man's self-confessed arrogance knew no bounds! she decided as she sent one of her hands on a quick foray of her own body to discover just how naked she was.

She was very—very naked.

'Did you know you have developed a habit of talking in your sleep?' he said suddenly.

Catherine froze beside him. She heard a very muddled and very disjointed echo of words being spoken by her that should have taken place in the privacy of her head.

Regretful words about Marcus.

'Shut up,' she gasped, terrified of what was coming. 'He must be quite something, this man you weep for.' He ignored her advice in the dulcet tones of one readying for battle. 'To reach the frozen wastelands where your heart lies hidden. Maybe I should take the trouble to meet him, see what he's got that I never had.'

'Why bother?' she slashed back. 'When you would never find the same qualities inside yourself if you searched for ever.'

'Is he good in bed?'

Her next gasp almost strangled her. 'Go to hell,' she replied, turning her back towards him.

As an act of dismissal it had entirely the opposite effect, because Vito's arm had scooped around her and rolled her back before she even knew what was happening.

And suddenly he was leaning right over her, all glinting eyes and primitive male aggression. 'I asked you a question,' he prompted darkly.

Her mouth ran dry, the tip of her tongue slinking out to moisten parted lips that were remaining stubbornly silent

because she was damned if she was going to tell the truth—
that she had never even been tempted to go to bed with
Marcus—just to soothe Vito's ruffled ego! Luxurious dark
eyelashes curled down over shimmering eyes as he lowered
his gaze to observe the nervous action—and completely
froze it as an old, old sensation went snaking through her.

He was going to kiss her. 'No, Vito,' she breathed, but
even she heard the weakness in that pathetic little protest.

It was already too late. His mouth claimed hers with the
kind of deeply sensual kiss that could only be issued by
this wretched man. It was like drowning in the most exquisite substance ever created, she likened dazedly as she
began to sink on a long, spiralling dive through silken liquid kept exactly at body heat so it was impossible to tell
what part of the kiss was hers and what part was his.

The man, his closeness, even the antipathy that was pulsing between them, was so sexual that she found herself
thinking fancifully of lions again. Her skin came alive, each
tiny pore beginning to vibrate with an awareness that held
her trapped by its power and its intensity.

Whether it was she who began to touch him first or
whether Vito was the one to begin their gentle caresses, she
didn't know—didn't really care. Because the heat of his
flesh felt so exquisitely wonderful to her starved fingertips,
and where he touched she burned, and where he didn't she
ached.

She tried to drag some air into lungs that had ceased
working, felt the tips of her breasts briefly touch his hair-
roughened breastplate, felt her nipples sting as they responded to the contact and moaned luxuriously against his
mouth.

With a sensual flick of his tongue, Vito caught that little
moan, took possession of it as if it belonged to him. And
as his hands worked their old magic on her flesh with the

sensual expertise of a master, he watched in grim triumph as, bit by bit, she surrendered herself to him.

'Does he make you feel like this, *cara*?' he grated with electric timing across the erect tip of one pouting nipple. 'Can he send you this far, this fast?' he demanded as his fingers, so excruciatingly knowing, slid a delicate caress over her sex.

She shuddered, moaned again, flexed and unflexed muscles that were moving to their own rhythm. 'Vito,' she breathed, as if her very life depended on her saying that name.

'Yes,' he hissed. 'Vito,' he repeated in rough-toned satisfaction. 'Who touches you—here—and you go up in flames for me.'

She went wild then. Three years of abstinence was no defence against what he could do for her. She moved for him, breathed for him, writhed and begged for him.

His laugh of black triumph accompanied the first deep penetrating thrust of his body. But Catherine was too busy exalting in the power of his passion to care that he seemed to be taunting her surrender. And as Vito gritted his teeth and began to ride her his eyes remained fixed on her shuttered eyelids, because he knew her so well and did not want to miss that moment when those eyelids flicked upwards just before she shot into violent orgasm.

Then let him see if she was shocked to find *his* dark face bearing down on her instead of her damned lover's face! 'Me,' he muttered tautly as he grappled with his own soaring need to surrender. 'Vito,' he gritted.

Why? Because despite what he was telling himself the very last thing he needed right now was Catherine shattering his ego by expecting it to be another man making her feel this good!

So he repeated his name. 'Vito, *cara*.' And kept on repeating it with each powerful thrust of his powerful frame,

'Vittorio—Adriano—Lucio—Giordani,' in the most seductive accent ever created.

Her answering whimper caught him in mid-thrust. Her eyes flicked open. She looked straight at him. *'Pidoccio,'* she said, then shot into a flailing orgasm.

They lay there afterwards, sweat-soaked, panting, utterly spent. He on his back, with his arm covering his face, she on her side, curled right away from him. 'Louse,' she whispered again—in English this time.

She was right and he was. So he didn't deny it. 'You are *my* wife,' Vito stated flatly. 'Our separation is now officially over. So take my advice and be careful, *cara*, who you dream about in future.'

That was all. Nothing else needed to be added to that. Catherine had unwittingly struck at the very centre of his pride when she'd mumbled mixed-up words about Marcus in her sleep. The experience just now had not been performed for mere sexual gratification's sake, but in sheer revenge.

Naples was shimmering beneath a haze of heat that made Catherine glad they were taking the coast road towards Mergellina then on to Capo Posillipo, where most of the upper echelons of Neapolitan society had their residences.

Vito was driving them in an open-top red Mercedes Cabriolet that must be a recent buy judging by the newness of the cream leather. And driving alfresco like this beat air-conditioned luxury any day, to Catherine's way of thinking. She could feel the breeze in her hair and the sun on her skin, and if it hadn't been for the man beside her she would have been enjoying this. The views were every bit as spectacular as she'd remembered them to be. And Santo was safely strapped into the rear seat, happily singing away to himself in whichever language took his fancy.

The three of them must look the perfect family, she mused. But they weren't.

In fact she and Vito had hardly swapped three words with each other since they got up this morning. He'd risen first, rolling out of the bed and striding off to the bathroom very early—but then he always had been an early riser. Catherine had stayed huddled where she was, listening until she'd heard Santo go down the stairs before she made any attempt to stir herself.

She'd needed her son as a buffer. Catherine freely acknowledged that. At least with Santo there she could try to behave with some normality. But Vito had been as withdrawn and reticent as she had been, as if his behaviour last night had pleased him as little as it had done Catherine.

'...sunglasses in the glove compartment.'

Catching only the tail end of Vito's blunt-edged comment brought her face automatically swinging around from the view to find him looking directly at her. Blinking uncomfortably, she turned quickly away again.

It was all right for him, she thought as she leant forward to open the door to the glove box, his eyes were already hidden behind silver-framed dark lenses, but he hadn't been able to look at her before he'd put the darn things on!

Once through Mergellina the car began the serpentine climb on the Via Posillipo. As Catherine turned her attention to enjoying the spectacular view now unfolding beneath them, a flash of gold caught her eye.

It was Vito's wedding ring, gleaming in the sunlight where his fingers were hooked loosely around the steering wheel. Glancing down at her lap, she saw her own slender white fingers suddenly looked distinctly bare. In what had been meant to be a dramatically expressive gesture she had left her rings behind when she left Vito all those years ago.

But now she shifted uncomfortably, a sudden wistfulness

sending her thumbpad on a stroke of the empty space where her rings should be.

'Do you want them back?'

Catherine jumped, severely jolted by the fact that he wasn't only looking at her now, but was doing it enough to miss nothing!

'It seems—practical,' she said, using the same flat tone as he. 'To avoid any—speculation. For Santo's sake.'

For Santo's sake. She grimaced at the weakness of her excuse, and even though she didn't check she knew that Vito was grimacing too. Because they both knew that if she put her rings back on she would be doing it for her own sake.

Pride being another sin they were all victim to in different ways. And her pride wanted her to wear the traditional seal of office that stated clearly her position in Vito's life. That way she could hold her head up and outface her critics—of which she expected to meet many—and feel no need to explain her arrival back to those people who probably believed their marriage had been dissolved long ago.

The car moved on up the hillside, and the higher it went the bigger the residential properties became and the more extensive and secluded became the land surrounding them. As they reached a pair of lattice iron gates that automatically swung open as they approached them, Catherine's attention turned outwards again, her interest picking up as she viewed the familiar tree-lined approach to her old home and found herself watching breathlessly for the house itself to come into view.

The gardens were a delight of wide terraces, set out in typically Italian formality, with neat pathways and hedgerows and elegant stone steps leading down to the next terrace and so on. There were several tiny courtyard areas fashioned around tinkling fountains framed by neatly clipped box hedgerows of jasmine and bougainvillea that were a blaze of colour right now.

As they rounded a bend in the driveway the house suddenly came into view. The Villa Giordani had been standing here for centuries, being improved on and added to until it had become the most desired property in the area.

Bright white walls as thick as four feet in places stood guarding an inner sanctum. Good taste and an eye for beauty had always been present in the Giordani genes. There was no upper floor terrace exactly, but each suite of rooms had its own balcony set flat against the outer wall and marked by a thick stone arch and balustrade supported on turned stone supports. The balconies went deep—deep into the house itself—in an effort to offer shade to their occupants, who might want to sit there and enjoy the view over the Bay of Naples, which was nothing short of breathtaking from this high on the hill.

In keeping with the upper floor, the ground floor kept to the same arched theme, only the low stone balustrades had been extended out to the edge of the wide terrace which circumvented the whole house.

Nothing had ever been skimped on in the creating of the Giordani residence. Even the four deep steps leading up to the terrace had been designed to add to the overall grandeur of the place.

The driveway continued on to curve round towards the back of the house, where Catherine knew the garages lay along with a stable block, two tennis courts and a swimming pool tucked away in a natural bowl in the landscape. But Vito brought the car to a halt at the front steps and shut down the engine.

Santo was already scrambling at the back of Catherine's seat in an effort to get out. 'Hurry up, Mummy!' he commanded impatiently. 'I want to go and surprise Nonna before she knows we're here!'

Climbing out of the car, Catherine unlocked the back of her seat to set her impatient son free, then stood watching as he raced off towards the house, bursting in through the front doors with a, 'Nonna, where are you?' at the top of his voice. 'It's me, Santo! I'm home!'

I'm home... Catherine felt her mouth twist in bitter rueful acknowledgement at just how much 'at home' her son had looked and sounded as his dark-eyed, dark-haired little body had shot him through those doors without a thought given to knocking first. And the words had burst from him in free-flowing Italian, as if it was the only language he knew how to speak.

As if he belonged here.

On the other side of the car, Vito stood watching also. And as her top lip gave a quiver in response to an unacceptable hurt she was suddenly feeling, he murmured, 'Here...' and Catherine turned only just in time to catch what it was he was tossing to her. 'A sweet to follow the bitter pill,' he drawled sardonically.

Frowning slightly, puzzled by both the cryptic remark and what he had tossed to her, she looked down to find that she was holding the keys to the Mercedes in her hand.

Her frown deepened, and for a confused moment she actually wondered if he was ordering her to go and garage the car! Then enlightenment struck. The sardonic words began to make sense.

He had not been watching their son; he had been watching her. And the sweetener remark had been a sarcastic reference to her reaction to the confidence with which Santo knew his place here!

But, worse than that, the keys had not been tossed to her to use to garage anything.

Vito was making her a gift of this beautiful Mercedes!

Her eyes shot up to clash with his, shaded lenses trying to probe through shaded lenses in an effort to try and dis-

cover before she responded if this was some kind of joke!
Out here beneath his native skies he looked more the arrogant Italian than he had ever done. The darkness of his
hair, the richness of his skin and the proud angle at which
he held his head all sent the kind of tingling messages running through her that she did not like to feel.

Sexual messages. Without her being able to do a single
thing to control it, the soft, springy cluster of curls nestling
at the crown of her thighs began to tingle and stir beneath
the covering of her thin jade summer dress. And her nipples
gave a couple of sharp pricking stings in response.

It was awful, like being bewitched. She even found it
shamefully sexy to note the way he had rolled up the
sleeves on his pale blue shirt—as if it came as supremely
natural for him to have them settle at just the right place
to draw attention to the hair-peppered strength in his forearms.

'I can't accept this!' she burst out shrilly—and secretly
wondered if it was the car or the man's sexual pull that she
was refusing to accept. 'It's too much, Vito,' she tagged
on hurriedly. 'And I have a car tucked away here somewhere,' she remembered, glancing around her as if she expected her little Fiat runabout to suddenly appear of its own
volition.

'It lost the will to live over a year ago,' he informed her
with yet more dry sarcasm. 'When no one else bothered to
use it.'

And when she still hovered there in the sunlight, so con-
ditioned to accepting nothing from Vito that she couldn't
bring herself to accept this gift now, she heard him release
a small sigh. 'Just bite the bullet and say thank you gra-
ciously,' he grimly suggested.

'As gracious as you were in offering the car to me?' she
couldn't resist flashing back.

His grimace acknowledged her thrust as a hit. And he

opened his mouth to say something, but whatever it was stalled by the sudden appearance of his mother on the terrace.

In her sixties now, Luisa was still a truly beautiful woman. Only slightly smaller than Catherine, and naturally slender, she was a walking advert for eternal youth. Her skin was as smooth as any twenty-year-old's, and her hair kept its blackness with only the occasional help from her talented hairdresser.

But it was the inner Luisa that drew people to her like bees to the sweetest honeypot ever found. There wasn't a selfish bone in her body. She was good, she was kind, she was instinctively loving. And if she had one teeny-teeny fault, then it was an almost painful refusal to see bad in anyone.

And that included her daughter-in-law, most definitely her son, and of course her goddaughter—Marietta.

'Darling, I cannot tell you how wonderful it is to see you standing here!' Luisa murmured sincerely as she walked down the steps and right into Catherine's open embrace. 'And you look so lovely!' she declared as she drew away again. 'Vittorio, the Giordani eye for true beauty did not escape you,' his mother informed him. 'This woman will still be a source of pride to you when you are both old and grey.'

Off with the old, on with the new, Catherine wryly chanted to herself. In true Luisa form she was discarding the last three intensely hostile years as if they'd never happened.

'Come,' Luisa said, linking her arm through Catherine's and turning them both towards the house. 'Santo is already raiding the kitchen for snacks, and I have a light tea prepared in the summer room. The special carrier bringing your luggage will not be here for another couple of hours, so we have time to sit and have a long chat before you need worry about overseeing your unpacking...'

Behind her, Catherine was aware of Vito's shaded gaze following them as arm in arm they mounted the steps. And there was an unexpected urge in her to turn round and invite him to come and join them. But somehow she couldn't bring herself to do it. That kind of gesture had no place in what they had with each other.

Yet...

With her fingers curling around the bunch of keys she still held in her palm, she paused on the top step that formed the beginning of the wide terrace.

'Wait,' she murmured to Luisa. And on impulse turned and strode back down the steps to where Vito was still standing where they had left him.

An excuse? she asked herself as she drew to a stop in front of him. Had she needed an excuse to justify coming back to him? Yes, it was an excuse, she answered her own question. And, yes, she needed one to approach Vito in any way shape or form.

'Thank you for the car,' she murmured politely.

He was gazing down at her through those dratted glasses, though in a way she was glad they were there so she didn't have to read his expression.

She saw his mouth twitch. 'My pleasure,' he drawled with super-silken sardonicism.

It put her set teeth on edge. 'I really do appreciate the thought,' she added through them.

'My heart is gladdened by your sincerity,' he replied with taunting whimsy.

Her eyes began to flash behind the glasses. Maybe he caught a glimpse of it, because his hand suddenly shot up and in the next moment both pairs of sunglasses had been whipped away and tossed casually onto the back seat of the car.

Stripped bare of her hiding place, Catherine didn't know what to do other than release a stifled gasp. Then, on another move that left her utterly floundering, he dipped his head and caught her parted mouth with his own.

His kiss was deep and very intimate, and his body heat was stifling. The way his fingertips were sliding feather-light caresses up and down her arms was just another distraction she would have preferred to do without.

But her lips softened beneath his, and she swayed even closer to the source of heat, and the shaky sigh that escaped from her was really a shiver of pleasure at what his fingers were doing to her.

'Now I feel thanked,' he murmured as he drew away again. 'And my mother is enchanted. That is two birds killed with one small stone, Catherine. You may commend yourself.'

'You sarcastic rat,' she hissed at him, stepping away from him with a sudden flush to her cheeks that had nothing whatsoever to do with pleasure.

'I know,' he agreed, still smiling that sardonic smile as he leant back against the car and folded his arms across his pale-blue-covered chest. 'But it was either sarcasm or ravish you,' he said, and when she blinked, he grimaced. 'You turn me on, hard and fast, Catherine. I thought you were aware of that. Watching you walk up the steps to my house was, in fact, the biggest turn-on I've experienced in a long—long time.'

'You're over-sexed,' she snapped, turning away from him.

'And under-used,' he tagged on dryly.

Catherine walked off back to his waiting mother with her chin up and her expression a comical mix of angst and sweetness. The angst was for Vito, the sweetness a sad attempt to show Luisa that everything was fine! But she dropped the Mercedes car keys on the nearest flat surface

she passed as she entered the elegant Giordani hallway—
and gained a whole lot of satisfaction from knowing that
Vito had arrived at the front door in time to see her doing
it.

He knew why she had done it. He knew she was discarding both him and his sex appeal—and the darn gift—
with that one small gesture. But, in usual arrogant Vito
form, he ignored it all, politely declined to join them for
refreshment and went off instead to find his son—which
was all that really mattered to him anyway.

Afternoon tea was surprisingly pleasant, mainly because
both Luisa and Catherine were careful not to broach any
tricky subjects. Afterwards Santo came looking for his
mother, so he could take her up to show her his bedroom.
They spent a while in there together, looking at and discussing all the surprisingly well-used things he had in there.
There was a nice informality about the place that touched
her a little, because it was really only a bigger version of
Santos's bedroom at home.

Home. Once again the word brought her up short. Home
is here now, she told herself sternly. Home is here…

After that Santo was taken by his grandmother to visit
friends he had in the area, and after watching them stroll
away hand in hand down one of the pathways towards the
lowest part of their huge garden, where Catherine remembered there was a small gate which led out onto the road,
she decided to fill in her time by making a tour of the
house, to reacquaint herself with all of its hidden treasures.

Nothing had changed much, she noted as she strolled
from elegantly appointed room to room. But then, why
mess with perfection once you'd achieved it? Most of the
rooms were furnished with the kind of things which had
been collected through several centuries, by Giordanis adding to rather than discarding anything, so the finished result

was a tasteful blending of periods that gave an impressive picture of the family's successful history.

Vito was proud of his heritage. And it meant a lot to him to have a son to follow after him. Coming here for the first time, Catherine had admitted to feeling rather in awe of the kind of rarefied world she was being drawn in to. But by then it had already been too late to have second thoughts about whether she wanted to marry a man who in name alone was a legend in his own country. Already heart and soul in love with Vito, *and* pregnant with the next Giordani heir, she'd had her freedom of choice taken away from her.

And there had been so many people very eager to remind her of just how lucky she was to be marrying Vito. He was special, and being treated as special had also made him arrogant, she thought dryly, as she stood gazing around the huge ballroom which still looked exactly as it had done in the early eighteenth century when it had been constructed. To her knowledge it was still used for formal occasions.

Her own wedding ball had taken place here, she recalled. It had been a wonderful extravagant night, when the house had been filled with light and music and laughter, and the gardens hung with romantic lanterns so their guests could take the air if they felt like it. A reminiscent smile touched her lips as she watched herself being danced around the vast polished floor in the arms of her new husband in her flowing gown of gold which had been specially designed for her.

'Have I told you today how beautiful you are?' Vito's softly seductive voice echoed back to her through a trail of memories. 'You outshine every woman here tonight.'

'You're only saying that because it flatters your own ego,' she'd mocked him.

She could still hear the sound of his burst of appreciative laughter ringing around this room even as she drew the doors shut on the ballroom. And she was smiling wryly to herself as she turned to make her way to the elegant central stairway. For Vito had laughed like that because the man *was* conceited enough to know that having a beautiful wife flattered his ego for choosing her, not her ego for *being* her.

That was the way it was with a Giordani, she mused whimsically as she strode along the upper mezzanine and in through one of the many doors that lined the elegant two-winged landing. To them, other people were the satellites which revolved around *their* rich and compellingly seductive world. It was supposed to be a privilege to be invited to enter it.

Enter where? she then thought suddenly, and brought her wayward attention to an abrupt standstill along with her feet, when she realised just where it was she was standing.

A bedroom. *Their* bedroom. The one she'd used to share with Vito before she ran away.

Her heart began to thud, her throat closing over as she took on board just what she had done while her mind had been elsewhere.

She had walked herself right into the one room in the house she had been meaning to steer well clear of.

Her first instinct was to get out of there again as quickly as she could! Her second instinct had her pausing instead, though, giving in to an irresistible urge to check out the one place where she and Vito had always managed to be in harmony.

The bedroom. The bed, still standing there like a huge snow sleigh, made of the richest mahogany and polished to within an inch of its life. The width of three singles, it still had the same hand-embroidered pure white counterpane covering its fine white linen, still had its mound of fluffy white pillows they'd used to toss to the floor before retiring each night.

Then she recalled why they'd used to toss those pillows

away so carelessly, and felt the tight sting of that memory attack the very centre of her sexuality.

Was that all to begin again? she asked herself tensely. All the rowing and fighting, followed by the kind of sexual combat that used to leave them both a little shell-shocked afterwards?

It has already started again, she reminded herself. And on that grim acknowledgement let her eyes drift around the rest of the room to discover that not a single thing had been changed since she'd last stepped into it.

Yet, *she* had changed. She wasn't the same person she had been three years ago. In fact, at this precise moment she felt rather like a lost penny that had found itself being tossed back, only to land in the wrong place entirely.

She didn't want to be here, didn't think she *should* be here, even though she knew without a single doubt that this was the room Vito would be expecting her to share with him again.

Not that she'd asked the question, and would not be doing when she knew it would only give Vito the chance to taunt her with the fact that she had been brought back here to provide him with sex.

Sex, lies and pretence—the status quo re-established for Santo's sake—and to slake Vito's thirst for revenge. She was about to turn back to the door when—without any warning at all—the bathroom door suddenly flew open and Vito appeared in its aperture. He must have come directly from the shower, because all he had on was a white towel slung around his lean hips and he was rubbing briskly at his wet hair with another towel.

His arrival froze her to the carpet. And seeing her standing there had the same effect on him. So for the next few pulsing seconds neither seemed able to move another muscle as shocked surprise held them utterly transfixed.

CHAPTER SIX

WAS he seeing her like a lost penny that really shouldn't be where it was standing? she wondered as she watched those lush dark sensual lashes slowly lower over eyes that were determinedly giving nothing away.

The silence between them stretched into tension, and within it Catherine tried to stop her gaze from drifting over him. But it was no use. She had been drawn to this man's physical attraction from the first moment she ever set eyes on him. And nothing had changed, she realised sadly as, dry-mouthed, she watched crystal droplets of water drip from his hair onto his wide tanned shoulders then begin trailing into the crisp dark hair covering his chest.

He was male beauty personified, his face, his body, the long lean muscular strength in his deeply tanned legs.

'Have your things arrived yet?' Deep and dark, and unusually sedate for him in this kind of situation, Vito's voice held no hint of anything but casual enquiry.

Yet her skin flinched as if he'd reached out and touched it with the end of an electric live wire. 'I…n-not that I know of,' she replied, eyelashes fluttering as she dragged her gaze away from him. 'I've been—showing myself around,' she then added on a failed attempt at sounding casual.

'No surprises?' he asked, drawing her eyes back to him as he began to rub at his wet hair with the towel again.

She watched his biceps flex and his pectorals begin to tremble at the vigorous activity. 'Only Santo's room,' she murmured, and wished she knew how to cure herself of wanting this man. 'It's nice,' she tagged on diffidently.

'Glad you think so.' There should have been a hint of sarcasm when he said that, but there wasn't. In fact he was playing this all very casual—as if the last three years had never happened and they shared this kind of conversation in this room all the time.

But then, wasn't she trying to treat it the same way herself?

The towel was lowered and cast aside. Catherine bit her inner lip and tried desperately to come up with some excuse to leave that wouldn't make her appear a total coward.

In the end it was Vito who solved the dilemma for her. 'Sorry,' he apologised suddenly, and took a step sideways. 'Did you come here to...?'

He was asking if she needed to use the bathroom. 'N-No,' she murmured. Then, 'Yes!' she amended that, seeing the bathroom, with the lock it had on its door, as the ideal place to escape to.

But it was only as she pushed her tense body into movement that she realised she was going to have to pass very close by him to gain that escape. And Vito didn't move another muscle as he watched her come towards him. So her tension grew with each step that she took, and by the time she reached him her heart was thumping, and her breathing was so fragile that it was all she could do to murmur a frail, 'Thank you,' as she went to pass by him.

'Are you going to take a shower?'

Her senses were lost to a medley of tingles, all of which were set on high red alert. 'Y-Yes,' she heard herself answer, seeing yes as good as no at this precise moment, when she had absolutely no idea what she was intending to do in there! She didn't even need to use the bathroom!

'Then allow me...' his smooth voice offered.

At which point she found herself freezing yet again as his hands came to rest upon her shoulders. Then his fingers began trailing downwards over her pale skin until they reached the scooped edge of her jade linen dress where the long zip lay.

Gritting her teeth, Catherine prayed for deliverance. He was standing so close she could actually feel his lightly scented dampness eddying in the air surrounding her. It was incredibly alluring, the kind of scent that conjured up evocative pictures of warm, naked bodies tangled in loving.

She shivered delicately when, with a deftness that had always been his, he sent the zip of her dress skimming downwards. By the time the fabric parted her shivers had become tremors, and she had to close her eyes and grit her teeth harder while she waited for the ordeal to be over.

But Vito didn't stop there. Next his fingers were unclipping the catches on her bra and her breasts were suddenly free to swing unsupported. And in all of their long and intimate association she had never felt so wary and unsure of his intentions.

Even the way he ran the back of one long finger down the rigid length of her spine was telling her one thing while his voice, as cool as a mountain spring, was telling her another when he suggested levelly, 'Make it a long shower, Catherine, you are as tense as a bowstring.'

Make it a long shower, she repeated to herself. Make it a long, *cold* shower, she helplessly extended.

'But of course,' he then added, and suddenly his voice was as silken as his wretched voice ever could be, 'there are other, much more pleasurable ways to cure your tension.'

And before she could react his mouth landed against the side of her neck and, like a vampire swooping on its chosen prey, he bit sensually into the pulsing nerve there that lay alongside her jugular. At the same time his hands slid inside her dress and took possession of her recently freed breasts.

Sensation went streaking through her. After the day-long build-up of sexual tension, it was like being sprung free from the unbearable restraints that had been binding her, though she did at least try to put up some kind of protest.

'Vito, no,' she groaned. 'I need a shower—'

'I like you just the way you are,' he huskily countermanded. 'Smelling of you, and tasting of you.'

He was already urging her dress to slither down her body, and in seconds she was standing there in just her panties. As those long, knowing fingers moulded her breasts so his thumbpads could begin drawing circles around their tips to encourage them to peak for him, his mouth continued to suck sensually on her neck.

It was all so exquisite, the caress of his hands, the wetness of his mouth, the way he was pressing her back against him. When he stroked one hand down the flat wall of her stomach and beneath the fabric of her briefs she simply gave up trying to fight it. On a shaky little sigh that heralded her complete surrender her eyes drifted shut, and, tilting her head back against his shoulder, she allowed him to arouse her in a way only a deeply familiar lover would arouse a woman.

But not enough—not enough. Her hands reached behind him to rip away the towel so she could press him against her, and her head turned against his shoulder, searching out his mouth so she could join her own with it. 'Kiss me properly,' she commanded, no shrinking violet when it came to her body's pleasures.

On an answering growl he swung her around, lifted her up his body until she was off her feet—then kissed her hard and hot and deeply. The wall not far away was a godsend as he pressed her back against it and let her feet find solid ground again. Catherine parted her thighs and pressed him even closer, then tightened herself around him.

He was very aroused, and with the towel gone it left him free to use other, far more invigorating methods to keep her riding high on the crested wave of pleasure. Dragging her mouth free from his, she tilted her head back and simply let herself concentrate on the stroke of his body.

'You're wearing too much,' he murmured sensually.

'I'll never wear panties again,' she agreed with him.

Vito laughed, but it was a hard, tense, very male laugh, and it set fires alight inside her that did nothing for her self-control as he caught her mouth again and began kissing her greedily.

'I need the bed,' she groaned, when things began to get too much for her and her legs threatened to completely give away.

'I'm way ahead of you, *cara*,' he murmured raspingly.

Opening her eyes, Catherine found herself looking directly into two hot, hard golden points of passion that were doing nothing to hide the intensity of what he too was experiencing.

And they were moving. Catherine hadn't even noticed until that moment that he was actually carrying her. They arrived at the bed. With a complete lack of ceremony he dropped her to her feet, then bent to get rid of her last piece of clothing.

As he buried his mouth into this newly exposed part of her body, she stretched out an arm behind her and began tossing away pillows, raking back bedcovers. It was all very urgent, very hectic, very fevered. No time for lazy foreplay, no hint of romance. She wanted him now, and it was patently obvious that he was the same.

As she lowered herself onto the bed, then began sliding backwards so she could lie down flat, she remembered the door. 'Lock us in first,' she whispered.

'To hell with the door,' he refused, following her onto the bed as if they were joined at the hip. 'I'm not stopping this if the whole house walks in to watch.'

With that he entered her, sure and swift, and as she cried out in sheer surprise he laughed again, the same very male laugh, caught her face between his hands then made her look at him.

'Hi.' He grinned, as her lashes flickered upwards. 'Remember me? I am your fantastic lover.'

He wasn't even moving. He was playing with her, toying with her. He had fired her up until she didn't know her own name any more. Now he was trying to lighten the whole thing!

With a flash from vengeful green eyes, she tightened the muscles around her abdomen. The motion made him suck in his breath. 'Want to play, Vito?' she taunted, and raked her fingernails along his lean flanks where some of this man's most vulnerable erogenous zones were situated.

The breath left his lungs on a driven hiss. Catherine put out her tongue and licked the sound right off his warm, moist, pulsing lips. He began cursing in Italian, and there was no hint of humour left in him when he began moving on her with a fierceness that sent her reeling away into a pool of hot sensation.

When she shattered her arms flew out, wide, like a swimmer floating on its back. Vito slid his hand beneath her head to her nape, then lifted her towards him. It was a need he'd always had, to capture her desperate little gasps as she went into orgasm, and Catherine didn't deny him them now as she breathed those helpless little sounds into his mouth and felt his body quicken as he too came nearer to his peak.

After that she remembered nothing. Not his own intense climax, not the swirling aftermath, not even the way he slid away from her, then lay fighting for recovery.

Outside it was still daylight. Inside the air-conditioning was keeping the room temperature at a constant liveable level. But Catherine was bathed in sweat from tingling toes to hairline. And beside her she could see the same film of sweat glistening on Vito's skin.

She watched him for a little while, enjoying the way he

was just lying there, heavy-limbed and utterly spent. Yet, even spent, Vito was physically imposing. A man with the normal potency of ten.

Potent...

Catherine stiffened—then went perfectly still, the sweat slowly chilling her flesh as she lay there, held by a sudden thought so terrible that her mind literally froze rather than dare let her face it. Beside her, sensing the change in her, Vito turned his dark head, then began frowning as he watched her steadily draining pallor.

But before he had a chance to say anything she sat up with a jerk, then began sliding frantically for the edge of the wide bed. Her long legs hit the ground at a run, her hair flying out behind her as she streaked like a sprinter for the bathroom.

Whatever she was looking for wasn't there, because she appeared again almost immediately. To say she was in shock was an understatement. White-faced, and shaking so badly that her teeth chattered, she looked at Vito, who was only just pulling himself into a sitting position.

'My things,' she shot out in a taut staccato. 'Where are my things?'

Still frowning in complete bewilderment as to what was going on, he shrugged. 'They have not arrived yet, remember?'

'Not arrived,' she repeated, then her eyes went blank, and Vito shot off that bed like a bullet from a gun because he thought she was actually going to pass out where she stood!

'For goodness' sake, *cara*,' he rasped. 'What is wrong with you?'

'M-my bag, then,' she whispered shakily, and when all he did was come striding towards her without bothering to answer she hit the hysteria button. 'My *handbag*, Vito!' she actually screamed at him. 'Where is it? My handbag—*my handbag*!'

It brought him to a stop in sheer astonishment. 'Catherine—what the hell is this?' he demanded, beginning to sound shaken himself.

She didn't answer, instead she suddenly burst into action again. Darting down to snatch up her dress, she began to pull it on. She was trembling so badly she could barely manage the simple task, but when he attempted to help her she slapped him away.

'I can't believe I let you do this!' she launched at him shrilly. 'I can't believe I let myself!'

'Do what, for God's sake?' he shouted back angrily. 'Make love?' He decided that was the only answer. 'Well, that's rich coming from the woman who just ravished me!'

If anything, her face went even whiter, though it didn't seem possible. And, on a pained whimper that did nothing for his temper, she turned and ran for the bedroom door with her fingers still grappling with the zip on her dress and the rest of her still completely naked.

'Catherine!' Vito barked at her in a command meant to stop her leaving the room.

But Catherine was already out of it and running down the stairs. Outside in the late-afternoon sunshine she found her handbag, still lying where she had left it on the floor of the red Mercedes.

By the time Vito had pulled some clothes on and followed her Catherine was just sitting there on the bottom step in front of the house, with the bag and its spilled contents lying beside her.

And there was such an air of fragility about her that he made his approach with extreme caution, walking down the steps to come and squat down in front of her. 'Are you going to tell me what that was all about now?' he requested carefully.

She shook her head and there were tears in her eyes. He sighed, his mouth tightening as he began flicking his gaze across the contents of her bag as if the answer would show itself there.

But it didn't. All he saw was the usual clutter of personal things women tended to carry around with them. Lipstick, wallet, the passport she'd needed to get her into the country. A packet of paper tissues, a couple of spare clips she used to hold back her hair sometimes, and a hair comb. He looked back at Catherine, looked at the way she was staring out at nothing, and automatically looked down, expecting to find the cause of all of this—trauma clutched in her hands. But her hands were empty, their palms pressed together and trapped between her clenched knees.

It was then that he spied it, lying on the ground between her bare feet, and slowly, warily, he reached out and picked it up.

It took him about five seconds after that to realise what was wrong with her. Then the cursing started. Hard words, hoarse words, words that had him lurching to his feet and swinging around to slam his clenched fist into the shiny bodywork of the Mercedes.

After that, he too went perfectly still, frozen by the same sense of numbing horror that was holding Catherine. And the ensuing silence throbbed and punched and kicked at the both of them.

Until a sound in the distance grabbed Vito's attention. His dark head went up, swinging round on his shoulders so he could scan the furthest corner of the garden, where a gate out onto the road served as a short cut to their nearest neighbours.

Then suddenly he was bursting into action again, spinning back to Catherine and stooping down to gather her into his arms before turning to dump her into the passenger seat of the Mercedes.

'What—?' she choked, coming out of her stunned stupor on a gasp of surprise.

'Stay put,' he gritted, then turned back to the house and disappeared inside it, only to come back seconds later with a bunch of keys in his hands. On his way past her bag he bent to gather in its contents; it landed on the back seat beside two pairs of sunglasses as he climbed behind the wheel.

The engine fired first time, and with the efficiency of a born driver he turned the car around and took off at speed down the driveway.

'Santo and my mother are on their way back.' He grimly explained his odd behaviour. 'I did not think you would want them to see you looking like this.'

Like this… Catherine repeated to herself, looking down at herself with the kind of blank eyes that said she couldn't see, as he could see, the changes that had come over her in a few short, devastating minutes.

Stopping at the end of the drive, Vito Giordani looked at this woman who had known more than her fair share of pain, heartache and grief in her life, and felt the air leave his lungs on a constricted hiss.

'How many have you missed?' he questioned flatly.

Catherine lifted those wretched dull grey eyes to him and a nerve began ticking along his jawline as he set the car going again, taking them not down the hillside but up it, out into open country.

'You can count as well as I can,' she answered dully.

Vito grimaced. 'I am afraid my eyes glazed over when I noticed that yesterday's was still there.'

Yesterday's, the day before—and the day before, Catherine counted out bleakly. A contraceptive pill for each day since Vito had come back into her life, in fact.

'I hate you,' she whispered. 'You've been messing up

my life since I was twenty-three years old, and here you are, six years on, still messing it up.'

About to remind her that it wasn't him who'd forgotten to take the damn pills, Vito bit the words back again. 'Getting embroiled in a fight about whose fault it is is not going to solve the problem,' he threw at her instead.

'Nothing can solve it,' Catherine countered hopelessly. 'The damage has already been done.'

Mouth set in a straight line, Vito said not another word as he drove them higher and higher, until eventually he pulled the car off the road and onto a piece of scrub land that overlooked the kind of views people paid fortunes to see.

They didn't see the beauty in it, though. There could have been pitch-blackness out there in front of them for all they knew. And they were surrounded by perfect silence. Not a bird, not a house, not another car, not even a breeze to rustle the dry undergrowth. In fact they could have been the only two people left in the world, which suited exactly how they were both feeling.

Two people alone with the kind of problem that shut out the rest of the world.

'I'm sorry,' Vito murmured.

Maybe he felt he needed to say it, but Catherine shrugged. 'Not your fault,' she absolved him. 'It's me who's been unforgivably stupid.'

'Maybe we will get lucky and nothing will come of it,' he suggested, in an attempt to place a glimmer of light into their darkness.

'Don't count on it,' Catherine replied heavily. 'Twice before we've taken risks, and twice I got pregnant. Why should this time be any different?'

Why indeed? was the echo that came back from the next drumming silence.

'There has to be something we can do!' he muttered

harshly. And on a sudden flash of inspiration said, 'We will drive to the doctor's. Get that—morning-after pill—or whatever it is they call it…'

Catherine flinched as if he had plunged a knife in her. 'Do you know what they call those pills, Vito?' she whispered painfully. 'Little abortions,' she informed him starkly. 'Because that's what they do. They abort the egg whether it is fertilised or not.'

'But you also know what they told you,' he reminded her. 'Another pregnancy like the last one could be dangerous.'

Her tear-washed eyes shimmered in the sunlight. 'So I abort one life to safeguard my own life?'

The anguish she saw in his eyes was for her; Catherine knew that. But she couldn't deal with it. And on the dire need to escape from both him and the whole wretched scenario, she opened the car door and climbed out.

Leaving Vito sitting there staring ahead of him, she walked, barefooted, across the dusty ground to a lonely cypress tree and leaned against its dry old trunk.

First she had almost lost Santo, due to mid-term complications. She had managed to hold onto him until he was big enough to cope outside his mother's womb, and the doctors had assured her that the same condition rarely struck twice in the same woman. But they had been wrong. And the next time it had happened she'd almost lost her own life along with her baby.

'No more babies,' they had announced. 'Your body won't take the physical trauma.'

No more babies…

A movement beside her made her aware that Vito had come to lean a shoulder on the other side of the tree. For a man who had only had enough time to drag on the first clothes that came to hand he looked remarkably stylish in his light chinos and a plain white tee shirt. But then, that was Vito, she mused hollowly. A man so inherently special that no one in the world would believe that anything in his life would ever go wrong for him.

His marriage had. From its unfortunate beginning to its tragic ending.

Catherine didn't count this latest encounter. Because in truth she no longer felt married to Vito; if anything, she felt more as she had done when she first met him: alive, excited, electrifyingly stimulated. Which was why they'd ended up in bed making love like there was no tomorrow. It was a taste of the old days—irresistible.

And now the piper demands his payment, she concluded dully.

'Santo needs his mother, Catherine,' Vito stated levelly—nothing more. He didn't need to elaborate. Catherine knew exactly what he was telling her here.

They were back to celebrating the living, she supposed. Santo needs his mother alive and well and very much kicking. Tears burned her eyes again. She blinked them away. 'I'll take the pill,' she said.

He didn't say anything. Instead he just continued to lean there, staring out at his homeland as if he was watching Naples sink beneath a sea of lava and was as helpless to stop that from happening as he was to stop Catherine from having to make that decision.

Without another word, she walked back to the car and climbed into it. Vito followed her, got in, fired the engine and drove them away, down the hillside this time, and into Naples proper, where he took grim pleasure in fighting with the unremitting flood of traffic before eventually turning into an arched alleyway which led through to a private courtyard belonging to his offices.

Climbing out of the car, he came around to Catherine's side, opened her door and helped her to alight. She didn't put up any protest, not even when he silently turned her around and did up the rest of her zip before leading the way into the building. His concierge took one look at his face and with only a brief nod of his head backed warily away, but his glance swept curiously over Catherine's dusty bare feet and tangled mane of bright hair as the lift doors shut them away.

It was getting late by now. The working day was over so the place was empty of people. Leading the way to his own office suite, Vito pointed to a door. 'Take a shower,' he instructed, and walked off to his desk to pick up the telephone.

As she stepped into the bathroom she heard him talking to his mother, making some excuse about them going shopping on impulse and forgetting to tell anyone before leaving.

It was as good an excuse as any, she supposed, so long as no one had thought to check their bedroom, where the evidence of what they had been doing before they went out was painfully clear to see.

The next call Vito made was out of her hearing. It was curt, it was tight, and it didn't improve his temper as he began his third call, instructing a fashion boutique a short block from here, that knew him through his mother, to deliver the full range of whatever they had in stock to fit a British size ten, including shoes and underwear.

Catherine still hadn't emerged from the bathroom by the time the concierge came in, laden down with the boutique's delivery. In any other mood Vito might have been interested in what he had got for his money, but since most of the items were simply a bluff to fool his mother, he merely told the man to place the purchases on the low leather sofa beneath the window, then dismissed him.

But before he went the concierge handed him a different kind of purchase entirely. It was small, it was light, and it bore the name of a well-respected medical practice in Naples.

Vito was still staring grimly down at it when Catherine emerged from the bathroom, wrapped in his own short white towelling robe that was way too big for her. She looked wet, she looked clean—and utterly miserable.

'I couldn't find a hairdryer,' she said, indicating her head, where her hair hung straight and at least five shades darker against the whiteness of her face.

'I'll find it in a minute,' he replied, walking towards her.

She wasn't looking at him, but then she hadn't done so since they'd made love earlier—not with eyes that could see him anyway.

'Here,' he said gruffly, and handed her the small package.

She knew what it was the moment she looked at it, even though her eyes couldn't focus on the writing. 'Two now, two more in twelve hours,' he instructed.

A cold chill went sweeping through her, turning her fingers to ice as she reached out and took the packet from him.

'I need a drink,' she said.

He nodded briskly and moved away. 'Tea, coffee, iced water?' he enquired, opening the doors to a huge drinks cabinet equipped with everything from kettle to cocktail shaker.

'Water,' she chose, then slid her hands into the cavernous pockets of the robe before lifting herself to take a forced interest in her surroundings.

This place hadn't changed much since she'd last been here either, she saw. Same classic trappings of a well-to-do businessman, same hi-tech equipment, only a lot more of it.

He turned with the glass of water. 'Catherine—'

'Shut up,' she said flatly, and, ignoring the grim tension

in his stance, she made herself walk over to the sofa where the concierge had placed Vito's purchases. 'For me?' she asked.

'Take your pick,' he replied. 'There should be a selection of everything you will require.'

'The man thinks of everything,' she dryly mocked as her fingers flicked open boxes and checked out bags with about as much interest as a hungry dog being offered a plastic bone to eat. 'Troubleshooter extraordinaire.'

He didn't answer, but then, why should he bother? It was only the truth after all. For who else did she know who could achieve so much in the time it took her to have a shower?

'I'll take these,' she said, choosing at random a teal blue silk dinner dress and some matching underwear. Going back towards the bathroom, she paused in the doorway. 'The hairdryer?' she prompted him.

He walked over to her, then stopped to silently hand her the requested glass of water that she seemed to have had already forgotten about, before he slid past her into the bathroom and unearthed a hairdryer from the back of a vanity unit.

Grimly plugging it in, he left it ready for her on the marble top, then turned to leave her to it. In her hand was the glass of water. The water was to help her swallow the medication he had given to her. He walked past her, then stopped, tensely swung back. 'Catherine—'

She shut the door in his face.

Fifteen minutes later she came out again, hair dried into some semblance of a style, her clothes looking unexpectedly fantastic, considering the way they had been chosen. The dress was short, slim, and edged with a layer of fine black lace. Standing staring out of the window, Vito turned when he heard her, then went still, his sombre eyes hooding over as they slid down her.

'Shoes,' was all he said, though, pointing to a pair of

teal-blue strappy sandals standing neatly by the sofa. Everything else had gone—where to Catherine didn't know, nor care.

She found out when they arrived back at the car and saw the back seat was full of packages. The car's roof had been raised, and as they climbed inside she felt the difference as a humid heat quickly enveloped her. Vito started the car and switched on the air-conditioning system, then they drove off, back home to their twisted version of normality.

It was growing quite dark by the time they arrived at the house. Lights were burning on the driveway, offering a warm welcome that didn't touch Catherine.

As they walked into the house Santo appeared, already dressed for bed in his pyjamas. With a delighted whoop he came running towards them. Whether it was deliberate, Catherine wasn't certain, but Vito took a small step backwards then slid stealthily behind her, as if he was trying to reduce Santo's options so he would run into his mother's arms and not his father's.

If it was deliberate then it was a very selfless gesture, one that showed a deep sensitivity to her needs right now. And an understanding that her emotions had taken a big enough battering today without having her son giving it a further knock by choosing to hug his father before hugging her.

So she received her warm bundle of love and hugged him to her as if her life depended on holding this precious child of theirs. And with his arms around her neck and his legs around her waist Santo chatted away about what he had been doing, with absolutely no idea that his mother was frantically fighting a battle with tears again.

It was only when she eventually set her son down again, so he could go to his father, and she saw the way Vito held Santo to him in much the same way that she had done, that she allowed herself to acknowledge that he too was suffering.

It was too much—much too much for her to cope with right now, when she could barely cope with her own inner agony. So she walked away, wishing she could just go and crawl into bed, pull the covers over her head and stay there for ever.

But she couldn't do that, because Luisa was waiting for them and expected bright smiles and conversation. Catherine played the game to the best of her ability, and even managed to smile at Luisa teasing Vito about the new wardrobe of clothes he had just bought Catherine because her own luggage hadn't arrived.

'But it came while you were out!' her mother-in-law laughingly informed them. 'How terribly impatient and extravagant of you, darling!' Her eyes twinkled teasingly at her son, and why were they twinkling? Because Luisa was seeing the gesture as a demonstration of how wonderfully romantic things must be between her son and his wife—when really things couldn't be more wretched. 'And what a lovely treat for you, Catherine...!'

Dinner that night was just another ordeal she had to force herself to get through. She had to eat when she didn't want to, smile when she didn't want to, had to make pleasant innocuous conversation when she didn't want to. And through it all she had to watch Vito watch her from beneath heavily veiled eyes, as if he was expecting her at any moment to jump up and start screaming the place down.

She didn't really blame him, for she knew that beneath her relaxed exterior she was so uptight it was actually beginning to hurt. She had been avoiding him like the plague since they got back. If he walked into a room then she walked out of it; if he went to speak to her she pretended she didn't hear. Now, across the dinner table, if she found herself being forced into making eye contact with him she did it from behind a frosted veil, which thankfully kept him out of focus.

But that didn't mean that she wasn't aware of *his* tension, or of the greyish pallor sitting just beneath the surface of his golden skin that had been there ever since he had handed her that packet in his office.

'...Marietta...'

Suddenly feeling as though a thousand sharp needles were embedding themselves into her flesh, Catherine blinked her mind back into focus on the conversation at the table.

'She was sorry she couldn't be here to welcome you home today,' Luisa was saying innocently. 'But Vito saw fit to send her off to New York on some wild-goose chase she insists did not really warrant her attention.' A censorious glance at her son gained no response whatsoever. 'Still, since Vito's priority had to be here with you and Santo, one of them had to go, I suppose,' Luisa allowed, with a little shrug meant, Catherine presumed, to dismiss her son's silence. 'She will be back by the weekend, though, so maybe we could all get together then for a celebratory dinner—which would be nice, don't you think, Catherine? The two of you were such good friends once upon a time. I'm sure you must be looking forward to reviving the friendship.'

'Excuse me.' She stood up with an abruptness that surprised everyone. 'Forgive me, Luisa, but I'm afraid I can't sit here any longer—'

'Aren't you well, Catherine?' It was a logical conclusion to make, bearing in mind that her dinner plate was sitting untouched, right in front of her. And at last Luisa seemed to notice Catherine's strained pallor, while, with the kind of good manners that had been bred into him, Vito rose gracefully to his feet also. But he was still watching her like a hawk, and Catherine wanted to scratch his blasted eyes out because he knew his mother had just advantageously stopped her from saying something she would have regretted later about Luisa's precious Marietta!

'Just tired, that's all.' She smiled a weak smile that was

really an acknowledgement of her own sense of relief at Luisa's interruption. For hadn't it always been easier to leave Luisa with her rose-tinted glasses in place than be the one to rip them from her? 'It has been a long day in one way or another.'

'Of course, dear,' Luisa murmured understandingly. 'And you are not used to our late dining habits—which probably accounts for your lack of appetite tonight...'

'Yes.' Catherine kept on smiling the wretched smile and bent to brush a kiss across Luisa's cheek before mumbling some incoherent remark about seeing Vito later as she stumbled wearily from the table.

By the time she had prepared for bed and carried out her most dearest wish by crawling beneath the sheets and pulling them right over her, she had hardly any energy left to do much more than switch her brain off.

So she was completely lost to a blessed oblivion when a pair of arms firmly gathering her in brought her swimming back to consciousness.

'No.' Her response was instant rejection.

'Be still,' Vito's deep voice flatly countered, and, drawing her into the warm curve of his body, he firmly clamped her there. 'You may wish to pretend that I do not exist right now, but I do, and I am here—'

'While your lover is several thousand miles away,' she tagged on waspishly.

'Marietta is your obsession, not mine,' he replied. 'But since you have decided to bring her into this bed with us, may I remind you that you are here to replace her? So stop fighting me, Catherine.' Once again his arms tightened to subdue her wriggling struggles. 'You may like to believe that you are the only miserable one in this bed, but you are not. And I need to hold you as much as you need to be held like this.'

He wasn't talking about Marietta now, she realised. He was talking about something far more emotive. Impulsively she opened her mouth to say something about that—then changed her mind, for her emotions were in such a dreadful mess that remaining silent seemed wiser at this moment than saying anything that could well start another quarrel.

So she subsided, reluctantly, into the warmth of his embrace, felt his muscles relax when he recognised her surrender. And as she began taking on board other things, like his nakedness against her thin cotton pyjamas, she bitterly wished that the man wasn't so physically alluring.

Wished to God that she wasn't so useless as a woman. She wished her heart didn't hurt so much and her brain was more able to make a clear-cut decision between what was right and what was wrong.

And she wished so very sincerely that the world would stop turning, so that she could get off it and never come back to it again!

'Cry if you want to,' his rusty voice encouraged.

'No,' she refused, but her body was already trembling with the effort it was costing her not to.

'It was the right thing to do, Catherine. The only thing to do.' Vito's mouth pressed a kiss to the back of her head. 'But that does not mean you must not mourn the decision.'

But it did—it did! And Vito was never going to understand what that decision was costing her because she was not going to tell him—or tell anyone for that matter.

'I just want to go to sleep and forget all about it,' she whispered thickly.

'Then do so,' he allowed. 'But I will be here if you change your mind, *cara*. Right here beside you.'

Was this his way of making up for the time when he hadn't been there for her? If it was then Catherine was not going to taunt him with it. Because she might be absorbed by her own torment right now, but she could feel the way his hands were tensely gripping her hands, that Vito was no less tormented.

CHAPTER SEVEN

HIS arms stayed wrapped around her throughout the long night. Each time Catherine swam up from the dark well of sleep towards reality she felt him there, and drew enough comfort from that to help sink her back into oblivion once again.

The next morning he woke her up very early and gently reminded her to take her second set of pills. Without a word she dragged herself out of the bed and disappeared into the bathroom. But it was only as she stood there in the middle of the bathroom floor, feeling a bit like a spare part that had no useful function, that the sudden realisation that something was different had her glancing down at her left hand—then going perfectly still when she saw her rings winking up at her.

The first one—an exquisite square-cut diamond set to stand on its own—she'd received a week after she'd told Vito she was pregnant with Santo. The second was the plain gold band given to her on her wedding day that matched the one Vito wore on his finger. And the third—a diamond-encrusted eternity ring—arrived the day after she'd announced the coming of their second baby.

When had he done this? she wondered frowningly, remembering that there hadn't seemed to be a single moment during the night when she hadn't been aware of him right there beside her. Yet he must have left her at some point and gone downstairs to his safe in the study, where she presumed he had placed her rings when she'd left them behind her, then come back upstairs to slide the rings on her finger—carefully, so as not to waken her.

But *why* had he done it? That was the much more disturbing question. And why last night, of all nights, when she couldn't have felt less deserving of these rings if she'd tried?

What kind of message was he trying to convey to her? There had to be some significance in him replacing these rings on her finger last night when things could not have been more pitiable between them.

A statement of intent? 'I am here for you, Catherine,' he had told her. And the appearance of her rings seemed to be telling her that he wanted her to know he was seriously committing himself to this ailing marriage of theirs, when really what had happened yesterday could not have been a better reminder as to why he was better off without her!

Guilt riddled through her. The guilt of a woman who knew she wasn't being entirely truthful with him.

But then, she asked herself, when had she ever felt that she could be? She had always only ever felt like a means to an end for Vito. First as a very compatible lover, then as the mother of his future child, and now as a necessary means of making his son happy. You couldn't build trust and honesty on foundations as shaky as theirs were.

Rings or no rings, none of that had changed since yesterday. She still felt as alone now as she had done on the day she'd lost their baby three years ago.

'Forgive me, Catherine,' he had pleaded at that time. 'If there was anything I could do to make the last twenty-four hours go away then I would do it. You have to believe me.'

But no one, not even Vito, was able to turn back time. It had already been too late for them by then. Just as it was also too late to change the consequences of the last twenty-four hours now.

And right now as she stood here, staring at these rings which seemed to be making such an important statement, she wished he hadn't done it when it only complicated a situation that was complicated enough already. Because he didn't know.

He didn't know...

A point which made her manner awkward when she returned to the bedroom a few minutes later. 'Thank you,' she mumbled, making a gesture with the hand bearing the rings.

He smiled a brief, tight smile. 'I missed them last night,' he explained. 'Then could not go to sleep without putting them back where they belonged.'

That word 'belonged' made her aching heart flinch. And for the life of her she couldn't think of a single thing to say in reply. So a tension built between them, a different kind of tension that lacked the old hostility that usually helped to keep them going.

Vito eventually filled it. 'So—what would you like to do today?' he asked briskly. 'I usually take Santo on a short horse-ride on his first day here, to brush up on his riding skills.'

'Fine.' It was her turn to flash a brief, brisk smile. 'I'll come too, if I may.'

But her light reply sent his eyes dark. 'That was the idea, Catherine,' he said soberly. 'That we do things together as a family.'

'I thought I just agreed to that,' she countered blankly.

'It was the way that you said it,' Vito grimly replied. 'As if you were afraid you may be an intrusion.'

This time Catherine's smile was wry to say the least. 'Let's face it, Vito. I wouldn't be here at all if Santino hadn't backed you into a corner.'

His eyes began to flash. And, snap—just like that the antagonism was back. 'Well, you are here,' he grated. 'And this is your home. We are your family and the sooner you come to terms with that, the sooner you will stop being an intrusion!'

With that, Catherine watched him slam himself into the bathroom, leaving her to wonder what the hell had motivated it.

Going back over the conversation, the only thing she could come up with that could have ignited his temper was her silence after he had explained about her rings.

Had he been expecting a whole lot more than a blank stare? A declaration of mutual intent, maybe? But why he should expect or even want that baffled her. He had never looked for those kind of declarations before when—marginally—they'd had something more substantial to work with than they had now.

And anyway, she concluded as she went to find something suitable to wear to go riding in, she felt more comfortable with antagonism than she did with the terrible lost and vulnerable feeling that she'd woken up with this morning. So let him stew, she decided. Let him bash his ego against the brick wall of her defences if that was what he wanted to do. Because there was no way that even Vittorio Giordani could really believe he had a right to expect more from her than he was willing to give out himself!

Yet something fundamental had altered inside him, Catherine had to admit as her first week in Naples drew to a close. For after that one show of his Italian temperament Vito had never uttered another harsh word to her, and seemed to be very careful not to give her the opportunity to flash hers at him.

He had allotted this week to spend with Santo, and work had been set to one side so he could play the loving family game their son had been promised. So they'd filled in their days by riding and swimming, and with trips out around Naples. And their nights had been spent in each other's arms, without even the slightest question of sex rearing its emotive head between them.

And slowly—slowly—Catherine had begun to relax her

guard a little, begun to cautiously enjoy herself. And without the sex to complicate matters, they had actually managed to achieve a kind of harmony that was almost as seductive as the sex used to be.

But it couldn't last. Did she honestly believe that it could? Catherine asked herself as she lay, supposedly relaxing with a book at the poolside, left entirely to her own devices for the first time since she had arrived back here. Luisa had announced her intention to take Santo and a group of his friends off to the beach for the day, and Vito had informed her that he planned to spend the day in his study, putting in some work for his neglected company.

Nothing particularly life-changing in those events, you would think, she mused to herself. But, for reasons she refused to let herself delve into, the book she was reading wouldn't hold her attention. After having pounded out a dozen or so laps of the pool, she had hoped she would just collapse on the sunbed in exhaustion, but she hadn't.

She felt tense and edgy, and kept glancing at the sky, as if she expected to find thunderclouds gathering on the horizon, which would explain this strange tension she was experiencing. But no hint of grey spoiled the perfect blue. In the end she gave up trying to be relaxed when she so obviously wasn't, and went back indoors to shower the suncream from her skin and get dressed with the vague intention of driving herself into Naples in an effort to kill some time.

She had rubbed herself dry, and was just in the process of smoothing body lotion into one of her long slender thighs when the bathroom door swung open. Standing there completely naked and with one foot lifted onto the bathroom stool to make her task easier, she glanced up, saw Vito filling the doorway—and knew in that instant that the storm she had been expecting all day had finally arrived.

It was a storm called desire. Pure and simple, hot and

hungry, tense and tight. It raged in the burning intensity of his eyes and pulsed in the tautness of his stance.

He was wearing a casual wine-red shirt and a pair of lightweight black linen trousers, but as his gaze glittered over her she saw his hand lift up and begin unfastening shirt buttons—and the frisson of response which went shimmering through her was electric.

She had to move. It was a point of necessity that she drop her raised foot to the floor so she could squeeze her pulsing thighs together. The shirt fell apart to reveal a wide bronzed breastplate covered in short, crisp devil-black hair.

'I w-was about to go out,' she heard herself stammer, really as a vehicle to break the raging tension now filling the space between them. 'Drive in-into Naples.'

'Later,' he murmured as the shirt landed on the bathroom floor. Then he half bent so he could slide off his shoes and socks before moving his attention to his trousers.

This was one hell of a strip show. Catherine clutched the bottle of lotion in one hand and felt her flesh begin to tingle. As the trousers parted to reveal that dark patch of body hair she knew thickened beneath the covering of his briefs panic erupted, though it was a very sexual kind of panic and had nothing to do with any dismay at what he was clearly intending.

Yet something made her put up a protest. Maybe it was the knowledge that the trousers were about to go, as she saw his fingers grip at the waistband in readiness to rake them down his legs.

'I... Vito, you—I—we c-can't,' she mumbled incoherently.

'Why not?' he countered.

'Y-your mother—Santo...'

But he shook his dark head. 'I've waited a full week for you to tell me it is okay for us to do this,' he said rawly.

'I am not waiting any longer, Catherine. I *cannot* wait any longer—'

Was that what had been holding him back for all of this time? Because he had assumed she would be rendered unavailable by the pill-induced menstrual cycle?

Chagrined heat blushed her skin from toes to hairline. Seeing it happen brought his strip show to a taut standstill. 'Is it okay?' he then demanded, and his consternation was so great that Catherine almost let out a giggle.

Except that this was no moment for humour. The man in front of her was suffering too badly to appreciate it—as his next gruff statement clearly illuminated. 'For goodness' sake, answer me, Catherine,' he commanded. 'The tension is starting to kill me, very slowly and very painfully.'

'It's okay,' she whispered.

Honey-gold eyes grew suddenly darker, their heat piercing her in all the right places. The trousers went the same way as the shirt, taking his underwear with them to leave only the man in his full and sexual glory to come walking towards her.

The tip of her tongue came out to moisten her lips as he took the bottle of lotion from her nerveless fingers then set it aside. And, without taking his eyes from her eyes, he bent his dark head to capture the tongue-tip between his own lips and draw it into his mouth in an act so inherently erotic that she whimpered in protest when he withdrew again almost immediately.

But his eyes continued to make love to her eyes as one of his hands slid around her waist while the other hand reached up to release her hair from the knot she had it twisted in for her shower. As her hair tumbled down over his fingers to brush sensually against her naked shoulders, he slowly drew her against him.

The contact was utterly scintillating, a fine brushing of warm flesh against flesh that set every nerve-end she possessed singing. Then he kissed her again, slowly and deeply, while stroking her with featherlight fingertips until she was breathless and trembling.

It was all too much for her to just stand there passive while he did this to her. With a sigh that was about as tactile as a sigh could be, she wound her arms around his shoulders, caught his head in her palms and began kissing him hungrily.

It was all the encouragement he needed to pick her up in his arms and carry her to the bed. The pillows went the way they usually did, to the floor, sent there by his urgent hands while Catherine dragged back the covers.

They came together in a tangle of limbs on the smooth, cool linen. It was all very deep, very unconstrained—very erotic, very definitely them at their most sensuously intense. Nothing was taboo, no means to give pleasure ignored—no words uttered. And their silence in itself was deeply seductive. Only the sounds of their breathing and their bodies moving in unison towards the kind of finale that stripped the soul.

Afterwards they lay just touching and kissing, communicating by all other means than talking, because words were dangerous, and neither of them wanted to spoil the special magic they had managed to create, that enclosed them in this wonderful bubble of tactile contentment. Of course they made love again several times during that long, quiet, lazy afternoon, then eventually slept in a possessive love-knot while the sun died slowly out of the room. This was fulfilment at its most sweetest.

Catherine came awake to find herself lying on the bed with a sheet draped strategically across her. Vito had gone from his sleeping place beside her, but her initial sense of loss was quickly replaced with a gasp of shock when she glanced at the bedside clock and actually saw what time it was!

Seven o'clock—Luisa and Santo would have been home for ages! What must they be thinking of her? What had Vito given as an excuse for her being so lazy? How could he just leave her to sleep like this?

'You rat, Vito,' she muttered to herself as she scrambled off the bed, then hurried to find some clothes to drag on.

The thin blue summer dress she had been intending to put on after her shower earlier still lay draped over a chair where she had left it. Scrambling into her underwear, then the dress, she was acutely aware of a series of deep inner aches that offered a good reason why she had slept so heavily. She had never been so thoroughly ravished!

She even felt herself begin to blush as she slid her bare feet into a pair of casual sandals, remembering just what they had done to each other. Or *for* each other, she then corrected, and on an agitated mix of pleasure and embarrassment she began finger-combing her tumbled hair as she made for the door.

The moment that she stepped out onto the landing she knew something was wrong, when the first thing that she heard was Santo's voice raised in anger.

What could be the matter? she wondered frowningly as she followed the sound of her son's angry voice down the stairs and into the main drawing room.

The sight that hit her eyes as she arrived in the doorway sent her still in dismay. Both Luisa and Vito were staring at a surly-faced Santo, who was standing there belligerently facing up to—none other than Marietta.

Of course it had to be Marietta causing all of this mayhem, Catherine grimly acknowledged as she watched the other woman bend at her slender waist to smile sweetly at Santo and say gently. 'But, darling, *you* told *me* that *you* would like your *papà* to marry me.'

'No, I didn't.' Santo angrily denied it. 'Why would I say that when I don't even like you?'

'Santino!' his father cautioned sternly. 'Apologise—now!'

If Catherine thought Santo had been difficult enough during the week before Vito arrived, when she'd endured some spectacular tantrums from him, she was now seeing he had not even got started.

For his face was hot, his eyes aflame, and his stance was more than ready for combat. Turning his glare on his father, he spat, 'No!' with enough force to make Vito stiffen. 'She's lying, and I won't let her!'

'Oh, please...' It was Luisa who tried to play peacemaker, by hurrying forward in an attempt to put herself between Santo and Vito. 'This is just a silly misunderstanding that has got out of hand,' she said anxiously. 'Please don't be alarmed by it, Vito.'

'Alarmed?' Vito bit out. 'Will you explain to me, then, why I walk in this room to the alarming sounds of my son being rude to a guest in this house?'

'A language thing, obviously,' his mother suggested. 'Marietta said something to Santo the last time he was here that he clearly misunderstood, and he said something to Marietta that she misunderstood. Such a silly thing to get fired up about.'

'I didn't misunderstand,' Santo insisted.

'Santino!' Vito turned his attention back to his son. Everyone had been talking in Italian until that point, but Vito's next sentence was delivered in clear, crisp English. 'You will apologise to Marietta now! Do you understand that?'

The little boy was close to tears; Catherine could see that, even though he was determined to face the whole thing out with an intransigence that was promising to be his downfall.

'Oh, don't make him do that, Vito.' It was Marietta who came to Santo's rescue. Marietta sounding beautifully placating. 'He meant no offence. He's just a little angry because I corrected his Italian.'

'No, you didn't!' the little boy protested. 'You said I was a nuisance and that when *papà* married you he wouldn't want me any more! And I hate you, Papà!' he turned to shout at his father. 'And I won't say sorry! I won't—I won't—I won't!'

Shocked surprise at his son's vehemence hardened Vito's face. 'Then you—'

'Santo,' Catherine said quietly, over whatever Vito had been about to say to him, and brought all four pairs of eyes swinging around in her direction.

And if Catherine had never been made to feel like the poor relation in this house before, she was certainly feeling that way now, as she stood there in her scrap of cheap cotton and took in with one brief, cold glance Marietta, looking smooth and sleek and faultlessly exquisite in her shiny black dress and shiny black shoes and with her shiny black hair stroking over one shoulder.

'Oh, Catherine!' It was poor, anxious Luisa that burst into speech. 'What must you be thinking?'

'I am thinking that this—altercation seems to be very lopsided,' she answered, without taking her eyes from her belligerent son. Silently she held out a hand to him, and with that simple gesture brought him running to her.

Vito was glaring at her for overriding his authority. Luisa was wringing her hands because her peaceful little haven had been shattered and she never could cope with that. And Marietta watched sympathetically as Catherine knelt down so her face was at her son's level.

'Santo, were you rude to Marietta?' She quietly requested his opinion.

He dropped his eyes. 'Yes,' he mumbled truculently.

'And do you think that deserves an apology?'

The dark head shook, then came back up, and Catherine

could see that the tears were real now in big brown eyes. 'I never said what she said I did, Mummy,' he whispered pleadingly. 'I just wouldn't,' he added simply. 'I *like* Papà being married to you.'

Catherine nodded. As far as she was concerned Santo had stated it as honestly as he knew how and the conflict was now over, because she was not going to make her son apologise to a woman she knew from personal experience could twist any situation round to suit her own purposes.

'Then you go off to your room,' she told Santo. 'And I'll come and see you there in a few minutes.'

'Catherine—' Vito wanted to protest, seeing his influence being thoroughly undermined here, but Catherine continued to ignore him as she came upright and sent her son off without offering anyone the chance to do anything about it.

When she turned to face all of those that were left, she found three completely different expressions being aimed right back at her. Vito—angry. Luisa—upset. And Marietta—smiling like a cat who'd pinched the last of the cream.

And why not? Catherine allowed. Within minutes of arriving here she had managed to stir up trouble between every single one of them.

'Good grief, Catherine, what a temper your son has!' Marietta broke the silence with a mocking little laugh. 'Sadly, I seem to have a knack of inadvertently sparking it off! I shall attempt to stay out of his way while I am staying here,' she determined ruefully.

Staying here? Catherine turned to look at Vito, who was looking as puzzled as she was by the comment.

'Marietta arrived home from the States this morning to find her apartment under water,' Luisa jumped in hurriedly. 'A burst water pipe while she was away has ruined everything, so of course I invited her to stay here while the repair work is being done.'

Of course, Catherine parodied, feeling an old-remembered weariness begin to settle over her like a thick black cloud.

'I have just placed my things in the rooms next to Vito's rooms,' Marietta inserted sweetly. 'If you want to know where to find me.'

'No.'

The harsh negative did not come from Catherine's lips, though it very well could have done, since she was thinking the exact same thing as Vito obviously was by the way he had stiffened his stance. Was he remembering a conversation they'd had recently, where the question of which rooms Marietta used when she stayed here had been the one of too many points of conflict between the two of them?

The woman had a special knack of making other people out to be liars.

'Whoever put you there has made a mistake,' he said tersely. 'If you need to stay here, Marietta, then stay in my mother's wing of the house. Catherine and I desire our privacy.'

'Of course,' Marietta instantly conceded. 'I will move rooms immediately. And I apologise that Luisa and I did not take into consideration the—newness of your reconciliation when we chose my rooms.'

And the poison barbs fly thick and fast, Catherine observed as Luisa began to look anxious again, which made her wonder if her mother-in-law had had any say at all in which room Marietta had chosen to use.

On top of that, Vito was getting really touchy now, she noted, as his frown deepened into a real scowl. First his son had annoyed him, then his wife by interfering, and now his mother, by placing Marietta where he didn't want her to be.

In fact the only person he did not seem cross with was dear Marietta. Clever girl, Catherine silently commended her as Marietta deftly flipped the conversation over to business things and proceeded to dominate his attention to the exclusion of everyone else.

Catherine left them to it to go in search of her son, whom she found sitting slouched over a large box of building blocks from where he was picking one up at random then throwing it sullenly back into the pile.

Chivvying him up with a determined brightness aimed to overlay the ugliness of the scene downstairs, she helped him with his bath then curled up on the bed beside him to read a couple of his favourite stories to him. Then, when she saw his eyes begin to droop, she kissed him gently goodnight and got up to leave.

'I don't like Marietta,' he mumbled suddenly. 'She's always spoiling things.'

Out of the mouths of babes, Catherine thought dryly.

'Do you like her?' he shot at her.

Well, do I lie or tell the truth? she wondered ruefully. And on a deep breath admitted, 'No. But Nonna does. So for Nonna's sake we have to be nice to her, okay?'

'Okay,' he agreed, but very reluctantly. 'But will you tell Papà for me that I'm sorry I shouted at him? I don't think he likes me now.'

'You can tell me yourself,' a voice said from the doorway.

They both glanced around to find Vito leaning there, looking as if he had been standing like that for ever—which probably meant he had overheard everything.

A quick glance at his face as she walked towards him told Catherine he didn't look pleased. But then, who did around here? she wondered grimly.

'We need to talk,' he murmured as she reached him.

'You just bet we do,' she replied. And once again the mutual antagonism was rife between them. Whatever they had managed to achieve in bed today had now been almost wiped away by one very clever lady.

They met in their bedroom when it was time to change for dinner. Catherine was already there, waiting for him when he came through the door with all guns blazing.

'Right,' he fired at her. 'What the hell did you think you were doing undermining my authority over Santo like that?'

'And what the hell did you think *you* were doing forcing him to take no other stand in front of everyone?' she shot right back.

'The boy was rude,' Vito gritted unapologetically.

'Our *son* was upset!' Catherine snapped. 'Have you any idea how it must have felt to him to have his own words twisted around like that?'

'Maybe he was the one who did the twisting, Catherine,' Vito grimly pointed out. 'Marietta was only trying to make pleasant conversation with him and...'

Catherine stopped listening. She'd heard more than enough as it was. On an angry twist of her heel she turned and walked out onto the balcony, leaving Vito talking to fresh air.

Out here the air was warm, after the air-conditioned coolness of the bedroom, and tiptoe quiet—soothing in its own way. Leaning her forearms on the stone balustrade, she tried breathing in some deep gulps of that warm air in an effort to dispel the angry frustration that was simmering inside her.

Because the hurt she felt, the disappointment and frustration at Vito's dogged championship of Marietta, only made her wonder why Vito had gone chasing all the way to London when it was so very clear to her that Santo came in a poor second-best to dear Marietta.

Pulling the glass French door shut behind him, Vito came to lean beside her. He knew as well as she did that the earlier row was not over.

'You can be so aggravating sometimes,' he censured. 'Did no one ever tell you that it is rude to walk out when someone is speaking to you?'

'Which makes me rude and Santo rude all in one day,' she said tartly. 'My, but we must be hell to live with.'

His sigh was almost a laugh, his sense of humour touched by her sarcasm, which actually managed to cool some of the angry heat out of her. And for the next few moments neither said anything as they gazed out at the view.

It was fully dark outside, but a three-quarter moon was casting silver shadows on the silk-dark water, and Naples was sparkling like fairy dust on a blanket of black velvet.

A beautiful sight. A sensually soothing sight.

'Did you tell Santo off just now?' she asked eventually.

'No, of course not,' he denied. 'I apologised to him for losing my temper. I'm not a fool, Catherine,' he added gruffly. 'I know I behaved no better down there than Santo did.'

Well, that was something, she supposed. 'So you're both friends again?'

'Yes,' he said, but he wasn't comfortable with it all. 'Marietta's right,' he muttered frowningly. 'He does seem to have developed a temper—'

'Marietta can keep her opinion about my son to herself!' Catherine returned tightly. 'And while she's at it she can go and stay at a damned hotel!'

'Hell, don't start on that one, for goodness' sake,' Vito pleaded wearily. 'You know I can't stop her from staying here!'

'Well, either she goes or we go,' Catherine informed

him. 'And while we are on the subject of Marietta,' she added tightly, 'you lied to me about her.'

'I did?' he sighed wearily. 'When was that, exactly?'

'When you led me to believe that you would be marrying her after we divorced. But the question of marriage between you two was never an option, was it?'

'Ah.' Vito grimaced. 'Would you care to tell me how you came to that conclusion?'

'Marietta herself told me,' she replied. 'When she was forced into twisting Santo's words around to cover up her own lies.'

'Or corrected a misunderstanding between two people who naturally speak two different languages?' he smoothly suggested.

A shrug of her shoulders dismissed the difference. 'Whichever, it still means that our son upset himself badly over nothing, and you brought me back here under a threat that was a lie.'

'I did not lie,' he denied. 'In fact I told you quite plainly why I wanted you back here with me.'

'You mean the revenge for your hurt pride thing?' she said, turning to look at him.

He was already looking at her, and their eyes clashed with a heat that set her insides burning. 'Did what we shared today feel like revenge to you?' he countered very softly.

No, it hadn't. Catherine silently admitted it. But the only other alternative she could come up with for his motives was just too unreliable to contemplate.

So she changed the subject. 'But you did promise me that if I came back here, then Marietta would be kept out of our lives.'

'I never made that promise.' He denied that also. 'If you remember, Catherine, I told you that I *couldn't* make that kind of promise.'

She released a small sigh, anger coming to life on the wings of frustration. 'In the name of decency, Vito. A man does not keep his mistress under the same roof as his wife!'

'I'm not telling you again that she isn't my mistress,' he snapped.

'Ex-mistress, then. Whatever.' She shrugged. 'She should not be here and you know she should not be here!'

'I know that you are crazy, obsessed and just downright delusional,' he told her.

Catherine's chin came around, eyes flashing green in the darkness. 'Okay, so I'm crazy.' She freely admitted it. 'You have married yourself to an absolute lunatic with obsessive tendencies and paranoid delusions. Now deal with the lunatic's delusions before she does something about them herself!' she advised.

Despite himself, Vito laughed. 'Now I do know you are crazy, for admitting all of that,' he murmured ruefully.

'Comes with the hair and the green eyes,' she explained. 'I believe I can cast spells too, and ride on a broomstick. Which also means I can tell a fellow witch when I meet one.'

'Meaning?' He was still smiling, fooled by her light tone into thinking the other subject was over.

But the smile died when she said. 'Marietta. Wicked Witch of the North, complete with black hair, black eyes, black heart—and a yen for other people's husbands.'

'She has been a close friend of this family for as far back as I care to remember,' Vito reminded her. 'I will not, on that point alone, think of alienating Marietta simply because you cannot like her.'

And that, Catherine acknowledged, is telling me.

'What about doing it because your son cannot like her?' she therefore suggested.

'He dislikes what you dislike.'

'Ah, so it's my fault,' she mused dryly. 'I should have expected it.'

But what really annoyed her was that he didn't deny it. 'I refuse to pander to unfounded prejudice,' he stated firmly instead.

Staring out across the bay, Catherine's eyes changed from flashing green to winter-grey, as if they were absorbing the bleakness in the moonlight. So he wanted sound proof of Marietta's prejudice towards them? she pondered. Well, she had that proof, circumstantial though it was.

The point was, did she tell him? For the last time she had brought up the subject she had demolished him so utterly that she'd vowed never to do that to him again.

Then she remembered their son, and the kind of depths Marietta's obsession with Vito had forced her to sink to— and with a sigh that told of a heaviness which went too deep for words, she made her decision. 'On the day I started to lose our baby,' she began, 'I rang around everywhere looking for you. I eventually tracked you down at Marietta's apartment.'

'I know that.' He was already stiffening. 'I have never denied to you where I was.'

Only *his* excuse for being there had been to get drunk and find oblivion from his nagging wife. Marietta's version had been very different.

'Why, then, if Marietta *woke* you immediately, did it take you six hours after that call to arrive at my hospital bed?' she asked. 'The traffic bad, was it?' she taunted softly as his face began to drain. 'Or maybe you ran out of petrol? That is another male euphemism for being busy in bed with someone else, I believe. Or maybe—just maybe,' she then added grimly, 'Marietta didn't bother to pass on my message until she felt like it, hmm? What does that tell you about your precious Marietta?' she demanded—only to instantly withdraw the question.

'No, don't tell me,' she said. 'Because in truth I don't really care what it tells you, when really there is no excuse you can offer as to why you went from me to her that day, or why you weren't there for me when I needed you to be. But from now on when I tell you that that woman is poison where I am concerned, you believe me,' she insisted. 'And you keep her away from both me and my son or we leave here. And if that is prejudice, then that's fine by me. But it is also a rock-solid promise.'

After that, the silence droned like the heavy pulse of a hammer drill while they both stood there watching Naples twinkle. How much of that Vito had already known and how much he had been stubbornly hiding from himself was impossible to tell. But Catherine knew one thing for sure, and that was if he still persisted in standing in Marietta's corner after what she'd just said, then it really was over for them.

Okay,' he said finally, deeply—flatly. 'I will see what I can do about the situation. There are a couple of new ventures on the planning table at the moment,' he murmured—thinking on his feet again, Catherine made note. 'One in New York, one in Paris. Marietta would be the ideal person to oversee either one of them. But it will take time for me to set it up,' he warned. 'She is going to need time to clear any outstanding projects from her desk before she can go anywhere. And my mother's birthday is coming up,' he then reminded her. 'It will be her sixty-fifth and she is planning a big party here to celebrate. She will expect Marietta to be here for it, Catherine, you must see that.'

Did she? she asked herself. No, actually, she didn't. But she could accept that Vito had a right to protect his mother from hurt just as Catherine had a right to protect herself and her son.

'Two weeks,' he repeated huskily. 'And I promise you that she will be gone from this house and gone from Naples...'

Two weeks, Catherine pondered. Can I live through two whole weeks of Marietta?

Do you really have a choice here? she then asked herself bleakly. For she could spout out threats about leaving until she was blue in the face, but she knew—probably as well as Vito knew—that she was trapped here no matter what the circumstances, so long as this was where Santo wanted to be.

'All right, you have your two weeks,' she agreed. 'But in the interim you keep her well away from both me and Santo,' she warned him. And with that she straightened away from the balcony, then turned to make her way back inside.

'I did not sleep with Marietta the day you lost our baby.' His deep voice followed her.

'"Sleep" being the operative word there, I suppose,' she derided.

The harsh hiss of air leaving his lungs had him spinning angrily round to glare at her. 'Did I ever call out Marietta's name in my sleep while you were lying beside me?' he rasped out bitterly.

About to open the French doors, Catherine went perfectly still, understanding exactly where he was going with this. 'No,' she admitted.

She heard him shift his tense stance a little, as if maybe relief had riddled through him.

'Unlike you and your Marcus. At least you were saved that bloody indignity.'

'I never slept with Marcus,' Catherine countered stiffly.

On the next balcony Marietta sat forward, the new name being inserted into the conversation sparking her back to life when only a moment before she had been almost defeated.

'Funny, that,' Vito drawled. 'But I don't believe you. So now what is left of trust?'

'We never really had any to begin with,' Catherine denounced. 'You married me because you had to. I accepted that because I felt I had to. You don't build trust on foundations like those.'

It seemed he didn't have an answer to that one, because the silence behind her deepened again. So, opening the French door, she stepped back into the bedroom. Vito didn't follow her. In fact he remained outside, leaning against the balcony for ages afterwards, thinking—she knew not what. But when he did eventually reappear, one brief glimpse of his closed, very grim expression was enough to tell her that his thoughts had not been pleasant ones.

And what bit of closeness they had managed to find in their bed that afternoon had now been well and truly obliterated.

CHAPTER EIGHT

So DINNER that evening was a strained affair. Luisa clearly had not yet recovered from the angry scene with her grandson in her drawing room earlier. And the way she kept on looking anxiously from Vito to Catherine said she too was acutely aware that the fine peace they had all been enjoying since Catherine had come back here to live had been completely shattered.

Did she ever bother to ask herself why that was? Catherine wondered, and decided not, because to do so would mean Luisa seeing the faults in her wonderful family.

Even Marietta was unusually quiet for her. She spent most of the wretched meal seemingly lost in her own deep train of thought.

Jet-lag, she called it when Luisa anxiously asked her if anything was the matter. But she did briefly raise herself to attempt polite conversation with Catherine. 'I believe you have been working for Templeton and Lang while living in London,' she remarked.

Go to hell, Catherine wanted to snap. But she smiled a civilised smile and answered cordially enough. 'Yes. I originally trained as a legal secretary, so it was nice to get back to it.'

'And your gift for languages must have been very useful to a firm which specialises in European law.' Marietta nodded in understanding. 'Have we ever used them, Vito?' she asked.

Busy glowering into his wine glass, Vito seemed to

133

stiffen infinitesimally, though why he did Catherine had no idea. 'Not that I recall,' he answered briefly.

'That is very odd.' Marietta frowned. 'For I am sure I know them. Marcus Lang is one of the senior partners, is he not?' she enquired of Catherine.

'No. *Robert* Lang and *Marcus* Templeton,' she corrected, feeling Vito's tension like a sting in her throat as she said Marcus's name.

'Ah. My mistake,' Marietta replied. 'Still…you are going to miss the stimulation, no doubt,' she murmured sympathetically. 'I know I would not like to go back to doing nothing again.'

'I have some work to do.' Vito rose so abruptly that everyone was taken aback. 'Marietta, I could do with going over a few things with you before you retire, if you are not too tired.'

'Of course,' Marietta agreed, but she was already talking to Vito's back, because he was striding from the dining room.

She followed very soon after him, which left Catherine to smooth out poor Luisa's ruffled feathers before she too could escape to the relative sanctuary of the bedroom. And by the time she had undressed and crawled into bed, she was ready—more than ready—to switch today off by dropping herself into the oblivion of sleep.

So having Vito arrive only minutes later was the last thing she needed.

Presuming he was coming to bed, she lay curled on her side with her eyes closed and pretended to be asleep. So when his finger gently touched her cheek only seconds later, her eyes flicked open in surprise to find him squatting down by the bed beside her.

'Something has come up,' he told her quietly. 'I need to go into Naples to my office for a while.'

'Alone?' The question shot from her lips without her

expecting it, never mind Vito. And instantly she wanted to kick herself as she watched his expression harden.

'Yes, alone,' he gritted. 'And if you don't watch out, Catherine, your mistrust is going to eat you alive!'

With that, he levered himself upright, turned and walked out of the room.

She didn't blame him. And he was right about her lack of trust eating her alive. Because it was already doing it.

'Oh damn,' she breathed, rolling onto her back to stare at the ceiling. 'What am I *doing* to myself?'

You know what you're doing, she immediately answered her own question. You are tearing yourself apart over the same man you have been tearing yourself apart over for the last six years.

Hearing the sound of a car engine firing into life, she got up and walked out onto the balcony to watch Vito leave. She arrived at the balcony rail just in time to see his red tail-lights gliding down the driveway.

'I love you,' she whispered after him. 'Even though I don't want to.'

And miserably she watched those tail-lights snake their way down the hillside until they became nothing but red dots among a million other red dots. She was about to go back inside when the sound of yet another car engine firing caught her attention. Turning back to the rail, she watched a black BMW come around from the back of the house where the garages were situated.

It was Marietta.

Even though it was too dark to see from up here who was driving, she just knew it was Marietta, and that she had to be following Vito to wherever they had arranged to meet.

So much for my paranoid delusions, she thought, and oddly didn't feel angry, or hurt, or even bitter any more.

But then she had a feeling that she had no more hurt left to feel about what Vito and Marietta did together.

She didn't sleep much that night. And was still awake when one car came back up the driveway at around four-thirty. The other she didn't hear, because she had eventually fallen into a heavy pre-dawn slumber.

Sounds in the bedroom eventually awoke her, and, opening her eyes, she found Vito quietly readying himself for the day. But a swift glance at his side of the bed told her it had not been slept in. On that observation alone, she shut her eyes again and pretended that she didn't know he was there.

An hour later she came downstairs in an outfit she'd had for years. The classic cut of the calf-length pin-straight cream skirt was timeless, the crocheted silk sleeveless top a soft coffee shade that went well with her warm autumn colouring.

Walking into the sunny breakfast room, she found Vito and Marietta there sharing a working breakfast. There was a scatter of paperwork lying on the table between them, and Marietta was busily scribbling notes across one of them while Vito sat scanning the contents of another.

All very businesslike, Catherine dryly observed, very high-executive, with Marietta wearing her habitual black and Vito in tungsten-steel-grey. And, considering he was supposed to have been up working all night, he looked disgustingly well on it, she mocked as she watched his dark head come up at the sound of her step and his eyes narrow as they took in her own coolly composed demeanour today.

He knew the look. He knew the outfit. He even knew the neat way she had loosely tied back her hair with a large tortoiseshell clip at her nape that gave the red-gold threads chic without being too formal.

'Going somewhere?' he questioned, not pleased, by the sound of it.

Catherine smiled a bland smile. 'To re-establish links with some old contacts,' she replied, and walked towards one of the vacant chairs at the table as Marietta's dark head lifted and her eyes drifted over her.

'*Buon giorno,*' she greeted. 'So you mean to go back to work,' she observed, like Vito, recognising the outfit.

'Better than "doing nothing again",' don't you think?' she answered sweetly as she sat herself down, then reached for the coffee pot.

'Did I draw blood when I said that?' the dark beauty said. 'I'm sorry, Catherine, it was not intentional.'

Of course it was, Catherine silently countered, while Marietta turned her attention back to the business presently in hand across the breakfast table and began discussing figures with Vito.

He, on the other hand, wasn't listening. His whole attention was arrowed on his wife, who was now calmly pouring herself a cup of coffee as if this was just any ordinary day. But there was nothing ordinary about it. He knew it—she knew it. Catherine was angry and she was in rebellion.

'Santino is with his grandmother,' he said, over the top of what Marietta was saying. 'They are spending the day at the beach again.'

'I know. I waved them off.' Catherine smiled serenely and reached for a slice of toast from the rack, then the bowl of thick, home-made orange marmalade.

'Vito, if you—'

'Shut up, Marietta,' he interrupted.

Her lovely eyes widened. 'Am I interrupting something?' she drawled.

'Not at all,' Catherine assured her, spreading marmalade on her toast.

'Yes!' Vito countered. 'Please leave us.'

Marietta's expression revealed no answering irritation as,

on her feet in an instant, she obediently gathered up her papers and left them alone.

Biting neatly into her slice of toast, Catherine watched her go. But Vito pushed back his chair and got to his feet. A few strides had him rounding the table, then he was lowering himself into the chair next to Catherine's.

'I don't want you to go out to work,' he said curtly.

'I wasn't aware that I was giving you a choice,' she replied.

His lean face snapped into irritation at her very dry tone. 'Rushing out there and taking the first job that is offered to you just because you are angry with me is childish,' he clipped.

'But I'm not angry with you,' she denied, taking another bite at her toast.

'Then for what reason are you doing this?' he demanded. 'You have not once mentioned going to work since you came back here!'

'Myself,' she explained. 'I am doing it for myself.'

It was a decision she had come to at some very low point during the night. That there was very little she could do to change the status quo, so she might as well just get on with it.

Which was the reason why she was dressed for the city this morning. Getting on with it meant getting a life. A life outside the suffocating confines of this house, anyway.

'What about Santino?' Vito tried another tack.

Catherine smile a rueful smile. 'Santino has more people eager to amuse him here in this house than a whole school of normal children have.'

'He prefers to have his *mamma* at home with him. *I* prefer to have his *mamma* at home with him. What is the use of my providing all of this,' he said, with a wave of a hand meant to encompass their luxury surroundings, 'if you will not let yourself appreciate its advantages?'

'That is a terribly arrogant thing to say,' Catherine replied.

'I don't feel arrogant,' he confessed. 'I feel damned annoyed that you did not discuss this with me before making your decision. It is so typical of you, Catherine,' he censured, unaware that her face had quite suddenly gone very pale. 'You are so stubbornly independent that you just go ahead and do whatever it is you want to do and to hell with what anyone else may think!'

'I'm sorry you think that,' she murmured, but her tone said she was not going to change her mind.

Vito released a driven sigh. 'Listen to me...' he urged, curling his fingers tensely around her fingers. 'I don't want to wage war with you every time that we speak. I want you to be happy here. I want *us* to be happy here!'

'With you as the family provider and me as the trophy you keep dusted in the corner?' she mocked. 'No, thank you, Vito. I'm not made of the right kind of stuff to play that particular role.'

'That woman should learn to curb her stupid tongue!' he muttered.

A criticism of Marietta? Catherine almost gasped at the shock of it—albeit sarcastically. 'Don't you have some work to do?' she prompted him.

As if on cue, the door suddenly opened. 'Have you two finished?' a cool voice questioned. 'Only we have a lot to get through, Vito, if we are to catch that noon flight to Paris today.'

The air in the sunny breakfast room suddenly began to crackle. Catherine glared at Vito. 'You're going to Paris today—with her?' she demanded.

He looked fit to wreak bloody murder. 'I—'

'Oh—didn't you know, Catherine?' Marietta inserted. 'I assumed Vito would have told you.'

'I was about to,' he gritted—at Catherine, not Marietta.

'No need now, though,' Catherine pointed out, raking her fingers from beneath his as she shot stiffly to her feet. 'Since your ever-efficient compatriot has done the job for you.'

'Catherine—' Vito's voice was harsh on a mixture of fury and frustration.

'Excuse me,' she spoke icily over him, 'I have some calls to make.' And she walked towards the door. 'Enjoying yourself?' she asked sweetly of Marietta as she passed by her.

The other girl's eyes widened in mock bewilderment. 'I don't know what you mean,' she lied.

Catherine just laughed—a hard, scoffing sound that jarred on the eardrums—and left the two of them to it, with Marietta's voice trailing after her. 'Vito, I am so sorry. I just thought…'

Vito followed her. Catherine would have been more surprised if he hadn't. He found her standing in their bedroom grimly pulling on the jacket to match her cream skirt.

'Don't you have a plane to catch?' she questioned sarcastically.

His angry face hardened. 'Don't do this, Catherine,' he warned. 'Don't rile me today when I've worked right through the night and am low on sleep and on patience.'

'And where were you *working* last night?' she challenged.

'You know where. The office,' he said heavily. 'I told you.'

'Alone?'

'Yes—alone!' he snapped.

'What time did you come home?'

'Around five—why the inquisition?' he asked dazedly.

'Marietta left here straight after you last night and arrived back half an hour before you say you got back,' she informed him. 'Is that the standard time-lapse for secret trysts these days? Only it's best to know the form when I start some trysts of my own.'

'You think I was with Marietta.' He began to catch on at last. *'Madre di Dio,'* he sighed. 'When are you going to try trusting me?'

Not in this lifetime, Catherine thought bitterly. 'How long will you be away?'

'About a week—' He went to say more, but Catherine beat him to it.

'Staying where?'

'The company apartment—where else?' he sighed out heavily. 'Catherine, it was you who told me to keep her out of the way,' he tagged on impatiently. 'And that is exactly what I am trying to do!'

'Enjoy yourself, then.'

Wrong thing to say, she realised as he suddenly leapt at her. She was trapped in his arms before she could gasp. And his mouth, when it found hers, was intent on taking no prisoners.

Yet—what did she do? She surrendered was what she did. Without a fight and without dignity she let her head tilt backwards, parted her lips—and let him do whatever it was that he wanted to do.

The slave for her master, she likened, not even bothering to be disgusted with herself as her fingers turned into claws that took a grip on his head and she let the power of his hungry, angry passion completely overwhelm her.

And his hands were everywhere, yanking off her little jacket, raking up her top, and the flimsy lace bra she was wearing beneath it, was no barrier at all against those magic fingers. She started whimpering with pleasure. He laughed into her mouth, then reached up to grab hold of one her hands and dragged it down to press it hard against his rising sex.

'Now this is what I call enjoying myself,' he muttered,

as he transferred his mouth to one of the breasts he had prepared for himself.

As he sucked, and sensation went rampaging through her, the telephone by the bed began to ring. His dark head came up. It would be Marietta, telling him to get a move on.

'Answer that and you're dead,' Catherine told him, and to state her point her fingers closed more tightly around him.

On a growl of sheer sensual torment he caught her mouth again, sent her mind spinning, drove her straight back out to where they'd both briefly emerged from, while the ring of the telephone acted like a spur to every single sense they possessed as she slowly eased her grip to begin sliding her palm along the full throbbing length of him with the intention of finding the tab to his trouser zip—

He stepped away from her so quickly she barely registered what was happening. And as her confused eyes focused on the wicked grin slashing his arrogant features she realised why he had stepped away as abruptly as he had.

Or he would not have escaped without injury. Vito was well aware that his wife could be a little hell-cat when she wanted to be, and the grin he was offering her was one of triumph, because he knew he had just stage-managed his own very lucky escape.

'Hold that thought,' he commanded. And with one flashing, gleaming dip at the way she was standing there—looking utterly ravaged without the ravaging—he had the damn audacity to wink! 'I will be back to collect the rest at the end of the week.'

He was gone before she could answer. And as she stood there blinking bemusedly at the back of the door, unable to believe she had let him do this to her, the telephone kept on ringing with a ruthless persistence that was Marietta.

Yet what did she find herself doing? She found herself standing there loving the sound of that ringing telephone, knowing that Marietta must be seething in frustration while she stubbornly hung on there, waiting for one of them to answer. And also knowing, by the length of time it took the ringing to stop, that Vito had needed to take time to compose himself before going to find Marietta.

It ended up being a strange week all told. A long week that made her feel a bit like a bride marking time before her big day—though she was truly annoyed with herself for feeling like that.

The man leaves one decidedly provocative taunt hanging in the air and you respond to it like this, she scolded herself crossly. But it didn't stop her from feeling pumped up with a waiting expectancy which had her almost floating hazily through the ensuing days until Vito's return.

The man was her weakness, his body a temple at which she worshipped whether she liked it or not. Control was a no-word where he was concerned. It always had been. Weak of the mind, weak of the flesh and weak of the spirit was what she was.

So she tried very hard to combat all of that by throwing herself into a whirl of activity that didn't seem to achieve anything. She had lunch each day with old acquaintances, put out feelers about a job, then found herself in no rush to take one—though she didn't understand it, since she had thought a job was her number one priority if she was going to make her life bearable here.

Another thing she learned was that Luisa was no part-time grandmother. She adored Santo. In fact she loved nothing better than to have her grandson with her all day and every day. She *did* things with him, took him places with her, was always interested in everything he had to say. And Santo blossomed under her loving attention. Not that he hadn't been happy with just Catherine back in London, because he had been—very happy. It was just that watching from the sidelines how Luisa treated Santo made Catherine realise why Vito was the man he was. Luisa seemed to instinctively instill confidence and self-belief into Santo, and she would have done the same for her own son.

A son who rang home every evening religiously. Spoke to his mother, spoke to his son—and spoke to Catherine.

Neither of them mentioned Marietta during those telephone calls. Catherine wouldn't in case the wretched woman was there in the room with him and would therefore know that her existence worried Catherine. And Vito didn't mention her because, Catherine presumed, Marietta *was* right there with him and he didn't want *Catherine* to know.

Oh, the evils involved in feeling no trust, she mused grimly one afternoon while she was standing beneath the shower attempting to cool herself, because Naples had been hit by the kind of heatwave that even the air-conditioning system was struggling to cope with.

But it wasn't just the heatwave that had forced her into taking her second shower of the day. The real culprit for that was Vito. He had left her hungry, and hungry she had stayed. So much so that even standing here like this, with a cold jet of water pouring all over her, she couldn't stop her body from responding to the knowledge that he was coming home today. Her breasts were tingling, their sensitive tips tightly peaked, and a permanent throb had taken up residence deep down in her abdomen. And if she kept her eyes closed she could even imagine him stripping off his clothes to come and join her here.

So when a naked, very male body slid in behind her she thought for a moment that she was fantasising his presence.

'Vito!' she gasped, almost slipping on the wet tiles in shocked consternation. His arms wound around her, to hold her steady. 'You frightened the life out of me!' she protested.

'My apologies,' he murmured. 'But hearing you in here was an irresistible temptation.'

'I thought you weren't due back until this evening,' she said, trying desperately to steady her racing heartbeat.

'I caught an earlier flight.' He was already bending his dark head so that he could press his open mouth to the side of her throat. 'Mmm, you taste delicious.'

And you feel delicious, Catherine silently countered.

'The water is a bit cold, though,' he complained, reaching over her shoulder to alter the temperature gauge slightly. 'What are you trying to do—freeze yourself?'

'It's so hot,' she murmured in idiot-like explanation. But the blush that suffused her skin told its own wretched story.

He knew it too. 'Ah,' he drawled. 'Missed me, hmm?'

'I have hardly given you a second thought,' she lied.

'Well, I missed you,' he murmured as he turned her round to face him. 'And please do note that *I* am not too proud to admit it.'

'Only because you want something,' she mocked.

But he just laughed softly, then proceeded to show her exactly what he wanted. And as she wound her long legs around his body, while Vito loved her into ecstasy, she let herself smile. Because a man couldn't be this hungry if he had spent the whole week doing this with someone else, could he?

Because even though it was her mouth that was gasping out its little sounds of pleasure, she wasn't so mindless with sensation that she wasn't aware that Vito was trembling, that despite the rhythmic power of his thrusts he was struggling to hang onto control here.

'Kiss me,' she groaned, as if in agony. 'I need you to kiss me!'

On a growl, he did so, felt her begin to quicken as his

mouth fused with her mouth and sent her spinning into orgasm, and almost instantly joined her, their mutual gasps mingling with the sound of the shower spray.

Afterwards he carried her out of the shower before letting her stand on her own shaky legs again. She leaned weakly against him while he set about drying her, her mouth laying lazy kisses across his hair-roughened chest while her arms rested limply against his lean hipline.

They didn't speak. It didn't seem necessary—or maybe they were both too aware that words tended to ruin everything. So when he made her stand up properly, so he could dry her front, Catherine stood staring wistfully up at his beautiful face and wished she could dare love him again.

Wished it with all she had in her to wish.

'Keep looking at me like that...' his smile was rueful '...and you will be spending the rest of the day in the bedroom.'

'Santo is spending the day with his friend Paolo,' she murmured.

A sleek eyebrow arched. 'Is that your way of telling me that you don't mind spending the day in the bedroom with me?' he asked.

'Got any better ideas?' she softly queried.

It was Luisa who asked about Marietta over dinner that night.

'She remained in Paris,' Vito replied. 'But she will be back in time for your birthday party next week.'

No Marietta for another whole week. Catherine's mood suddenly felt positively buoyant. And remained like that throughout the next few days as their life returned to the same routine it had developed before Vito had taken Marietta to Paris. He spent his mornings in his study and his afternoons with his wife and son while his mother became deeply involved in the preparations for her party at the weekend.

In fact, life could almost be described as happy. They swam in the pool and took drives into the mountains in an attempt to escape the oppressive heat. And Vito took Santo and a small group of his friends out for the day so that Catherine could help Luisa. Then a job cropped up that Catherine quite fancied, because it involved working freelance from home, translating manuscripts for a publishing company.

'I must be getting lazy,' she confessed to Vito that evening as they lay stretched out on the bed together.

'It could not be, I suppose, that you are merely contented?' he suggested.

Is that why I've been working so hard through the last few years? she asked herself. Because I was so discontented with my life?

It could be, she had to admit, because she certainly hadn't felt this relaxed with herself in a very long time.

'Well, I am going to have to commandeer the library to use as my workplace,' she warned him. 'It's either there or your study, and I don't think you would like it if I moved in there with you.'

'We would neither of us get much work done,' he agreed. Then, 'Mmm,' he groaned. 'You are very good at this.'

He was lying stretched out on his stomach and Catherine was running her nails down the muscle-cushioned tautness of gold satin skin covering his long back while he enjoyed the sensation with all the self-indulgence of a true hedonist.

'I know,' she replied with a bland conceit. 'I've had loads of practice, you see.'

She'd meant with him, because once upon a time they'd used to lie for ages just doing this. But from the way his muscles tensed Catherine knew he had misunderstood her.

'How much practice?' he demanded.

Sighing, she sat up and away from him.

He moved too, rolling onto his back to glare up at her. 'How many lovers have there been, Catherine?' He insisted on an answer.

'You know there was no one before you,' she reminded him. 'So why start asking questions like that now, all of these years later?'

'I meant *since* we married.'

Turning her head, she looked down at this man who was lying beside her in all his naked arrogance, with the power of his virility on blatant display, and wished she knew what made his mind tick as well as she knew his body.

'How many for you?' she counter-challenged.

'None,' he answered unhesitatingly.

'Same here,' she replied, and knew they both thought the other was lying. 'Does it matter?' she asked.

'No.' He grimaced, and she knew that was a lie also.

Her hand reached out to lightly stroke him. Releasing a small sigh, he closed his eyes. 'Okay,' he said. 'I can take a hint. You can ravish me.'

Coming on top of him, Catherine eased him inside her then sighed herself. 'Talking never did us any favours, Vito,' she murmured sombrely. 'Let's make a pact not to do it more than is absolutely necessary.'

Then, before he could answer, she closed her own eyes and began to move over him. And she rode him with a muscular co-ordination that soon sent any arguments he might have been about to voice fleeing in favour of more pleasurable pursuits.

CHAPTER NINE

THE house was on show tonight, lit by strategically placed halogens that turned its white walls a seductive gold, and its many garden features were subtly lit from within the shrubbery that lined its many pathways. Inside, everything had been cleaned or swept or dusted or polished, and in the large formal dining room attached to the ballroom a buffet banquet fit for kings had been laid.

Which left only the house occupants to dress themselves up in the kind of clothes that would complement the house. Catherine had achieved this by deciding to wear a striking long red silk gown with a strapless and boned basque-style bodice that was as bold as it was stunning with her colouring. She had dressed her hair into an elegant twist held in place by a diamond clasp that allowed a few stray tendrils to curl around her nape and around the diamond earrings she had dangling from her earlobes. And on her feet she wore very high, very strappy, shiny red shoes that forced her to move in a way that set men's pulses racing.

It certainly set Vito's pulses racing as he watched her come gliding down the stairs towards him. He had just returned from delivering Santo into the care of Paolo's *mamma*, where he was to enjoy his first sleep-over.

Which did not mean he had missed out on the fun. Luisa had been all for thoroughly enjoying her whole day, so when Santo decided that she should have a special birthday tea party with him and his friends, his *nonna* had been more than willing to play along. So it had been a balloons and red jelly party, with a novelty cake and the kind of games children believed a prerequisite for birthdays.

149

It had been fun. Probably would turn out to have been more fun than the grown up party that was about to follow, Catherine mused wryly as she watched Vito watch her come towards him. And the dark gleam in his eyes was telling her everything she wanted to know. Pride and appreciation were the words that came to mind, underpinned by the ever-present sexual vibrations that were such an integral part of what they had always shared.

'You look as if you have just stepped out of one of my father's Pre-Raphaelites,' he murmured deeply as she reached him, then frowned. 'But something is missing...'

'Jewellery,' Catherine agreed, touching her bare throat. 'You have most of it locked away in your safe, if you remember.'

'Then lead the way to my study,' he commanded, 'and we will rectify the situation immediately.'

Walking off in the direction of his study, she could feel the heat of his eyes as he followed behind her, and her ruby-painted mouth gave a rueful twitch because she was aware that he was now able to see how her gown dipped at the back in an audaciously deep V to her slender waistline.

'Very provocative,' he drawled.

Casting him a flirtatious glance over her shoulder, she replied, 'I *like* being provocative.'

His answering laugh was low and husky as they entered his study. And he was still smiling when he turned back to her after extracting something from the safe. Expecting him to come towards her with her old jewellery box in his hands, she was surprised, therefore, when he held only a flat black velvet case. 'Don't I get to choose?' she asked.

'No,' he replied. 'And that dress is most definitely an outright provocation,' he added, again eyeing censoriously the amount of naked back she had on show. 'Make sure I vet every man you dance with tonight.'

Catherine mocked him with a look as he came to stand behind her. 'You're being very imperious,' she complained. 'Choosing my dance partners and choosing my jewellery. What if I don't like your choice—like what you have in that box, for instance?'

'Tell me, then, what you think,' he said, and with that deftness that was his, something cool and heavy landed against her chest.

She transferred her eyes from him to herself, and an instant gasp of surprise whispered from her as she stared at the most exquisite diamond-encrusted heart resting just above the valley between the creamy slopes of her breasts.

'Oh, but this is beautiful,' she breathed, lifting slender fingers to gently touch the heart.

'Don't sound so surprised,' he drawled as he concentrated on fastening the intricate clasp which would lock the necklace safely in place. 'I may be imperious, but my taste is usually faultless.'

'It's a locket,' she realised, ignoring his conceit. 'If I look inside will I find your arrogant face looking out at me?'

'No,' he laughed. 'It is for you to decide who you carry around in there.'

You, Catherine thought. It would only ever be his image he would find nestling in any heart she possessed.

'Well, thank you.' She smiled up at him, keeping the tone as light as it had been between them despite the sudden wistfulness she was feeling inside. 'Now I feel properly decked out to grace the arm of the imperious Italian with the faultless taste.'

She knew the moment she saw his eyes cloud over that her response had disappointed him. 'You've always been fit to grace the arm of any man, Catherine,' he informed her deeply. 'I just happen to be the lucky one who claims the right to have you there.'

It was too much, too intense. They just didn't share these kind of deep and meaningful discussions. Never had done, never would do. It was the way of their relationship.

Shallow, she wanted to call it, but shallow didn't really say it either. Because there had never been anything shallow in the way she and Vito responded to each other.

What they really did was muddle on, never knowing what the other felt inside, because it was safer not knowing than finding out and being mortally wounded. So instead they used their love for their son as the common denominator to justify their being together—and the sex, of course, which had never been a problem where they were concerned.

And maybe her own clouding expression reminded him of all of that, because in the next moment Vito was smiling again, and the mockery was back when he ran a long finger down her spine and allowed it to settle low in the hollow of her back where the deep V in her dress finished.

'I have this terrible archaic urge to send you back to your room to change,' he admitted.

Turning to face him, Catherine baited him with a look. 'Just remember who gets to remove it himself later,' she softly suggested.

Luisa appeared then, saving Catherine from a rather delicious bit of punishing ravishment for that piece of seduction. 'Oh, Catherine, what a lovely necklace!' she exclaimed when she saw it.

'I am reliably informed by the man who gave it to me that his taste is faultless,' Catherine replied mock solemnly.

'Vittorio, your conceit will one day be your downfall,' his mother scolded.

'And there was I about to say that I get my faultless good taste from you,' Vito sighed—then, quite seriously, 'You look beautiful, *mi amore*. How can a man be so lucky to have a *mamma* like you?'

'Now he is trying to use his charm on me to get him out of trouble,' Luisa confided to a smiling Catherine. 'It was always the same, even when he was as small as Santino.'

But she did look beautiful. A beautiful person dressed in shimmering gold satin who, two hours later, was wearing the soft flush of pleasure from the wealth of compliments that had flooded her way about her looking not a day over forty.

'She's enjoying this,' Catherine murmured to Vito as she caught sight of no less than three gentlemen gallantly vying for his mother's hand for the next dance.

'More than you are, I think,' he replied quietly.

But then, she'd had to outface a lot of curiosity from people she'd used to know three years ago. Not that any of them had been allowed to quench their curiosity about the present state of her marriage, because Vito had remained steadfastly at her side throughout the whole evening, as if to act as a shield to that kind of intrusion.

And with a hand lightly resting on the curve of her hip, so his thumb could make the occasional caressing stroke across the skin left exposed at the base of her spine, if she moved he moved with her; if she was invited to dance he politely refused for her. It was all very possessive, and deliciously seductive.

So the evening wore on, the champagne flowed freely, and the hired eight-piece orchestra played while some people danced and others went to help themselves to the buffet. And the only thing that seemed to be missing was— Marietta.

'Where is she?' she asked Vito.

'Delayed, so I believe,' he answered briefly.

'But your mother will be disappointed if she isn't here to toast her birthday.'

'Oh, don't worry,' he said dryly. 'I would say that you

can virtually count on her being here at some point or other.'

Catherine frowned, not liking the abrasion she had caught in his tone when he'd said that. In fact, when she thought about it, Vito's tone had been distinctly abrasive whenever Marietta's name had come up since their trip to Paris.

Had they had a row? she wondered. Then felt something disturbingly like hope curl her stomach. Had Vito actually come to accept that if he wanted his marriage to succeed this time then it had to be without Marietta in its shadows, and had he already called the parting of the ways he had promised?

Hope was a seed that could bloom all too quickly when its host was so eager to feed it. And Catherine was more than ready to do that tonight, with her man behaving so very possessively and with his diamond heart lying against the warm skin just above her breasts.

Good or bad timing on his part that he sent that intrusive thumbpad of his skating across the triangle of flesh exposed by the V of her gown? Whatever, she quivered, and she quivered violently enough to make Vito utter a soft curse beneath his breath.

'Let's dance,' he determined huskily.

It was an excuse to hold her closer. Catherine knew that as she let him guide her out onto the dance floor. His palm flattened against the silk-smooth skin of her back as his other hand closed around her fingers, and as she rested her free hand against his lapel he set them moving to one of those soulful melodies that had a nasty habit of touching the heartstrings. The usual vibrations that erupted between the two of them the moment their bodies were in touch with each other began to pulse all around them.

It was dangerously seductive, wholly mesmerising. They didn't attempt to talk, and the silence itself added fuel to their growing awareness of each other. When his lips touched her brow it was like being bathed in static. When his thigh brushed her thighs it set the soft curls of hair around her sex stinging in reaction.

And, in response to it all, she felt Vito's inner self quicken, felt his heart pick up pace beneath her resting hand and that familiar tension enter his body. Unable to resist the urge, she lifted her chin to look at him at the same moment that his lush, long curling lashes gave a flicker as he lowered his gaze and looked at her.

Their eyes suddenly locked. And for a short, stunning moment it was as if everything going on around them faded into the ether. It was seduction at its most torturously exquisite. He held her captive with eyes that were saturating her in the liquid gold heat they were pouring into her.

It was total absorption. Utterly enthralling. Because right there in the middle of a hundred other people she was sure she could feel love come beating down upon her from the one place she had never expected to find it.

'Vito...' she heard herself whisper, though she didn't know why.

'Catherine,' he said tensely. 'We have to—'

'Luisa. Happy birthday, darling!' a beautifully rich female voice called out in its warmest Italian and—snap— the link between them was broken.

Marietta had arrived. Dear Marietta. Even the music came to an abrupt standstill.

But then, if anyone could make a perfectly timed entrance, it was Marietta, Catherine mused cynically as she turned within Vito's slackened grasp to view her worst enemy.

At which point everything alive inside her froze to a complete cessation.

For there, framed by the open glass doors of the glittering ballroom, stood Marietta, dressed in a silver sequinned creation that was as bold as it was beautiful and did tremendous things for her wonderful figure.

But it wasn't what Marietta was wearing that was paralysing Catherine. That achievement was down to the man who was standing at Marietta's elbow. Tall, dark, extremely attractive in a very British kind of way, he was looking distinctly uncomfortable with his own presence here...

'Marcus,' she breathed, too shocked to even think of holding the name back.

So the tensing she felt taking place behind her sent her heart plummeting in a sinking dive to her stomach as she watched Marcus give a tense tug at his shirt collar before offering the hand and a stiff smile to Luisa, who was being formally introduced to him.

Marietta was smiling serenely while Luisa attempted to put Marcus at his ease, as you would expect from Luisa. But Marcus was beyond being put at his ease. It was so obvious he did not want to be here that Catherine could not understand why he was!

Confusion began to replace the numbing sense of surprised horror. 'But what is he doing here?' she murmured, bewildered.

'You mean you cannot guess?' Vito taunted grimly.

'It has nothing to do with me, if that's what you're thinking!' she protested.

'No? I would say that his being here has everything to do with you,' he coolly informed her.

As if to confirm that, Marcus's restless eyes suddenly alighted on her standing there, with Vito tall and grim behind her. And colour rushed into the other man's face. It was awful. Like watching, helplessly from the sidelines, someone slowly drown without being able to do a single thing to help him.

Then she caught the flash from a pair of malevolent eyes, and suddenly realised that this was all Marietta's doing.

Marietta had somehow managed to find out about Catherine's more personal association with Marcus and she had brought him here with the single intention of using that information to cause trouble.

But who could have told her? Her mind quickly tried to assess the situation. Certainly not Marcus himself. Besides his clear discomfort with his present position, he was not the kind of man who told kiss and tell stories.

And what was even more worrying was how Marietta was no longer attempting to hide her malevolence. It was out of the closet and on show for anyone to see—including Vito, if he wanted to.

Determined to find out just what was going on, Catherine went to break free from Vito. But his steely grip held her.

'No,' he refused. 'This is Marietta's game. We will let her play it.'

And he wasn't shocked. He wasn't even angry! 'You knew he was coming,' she realised shakily.

'It is very rare that anyone enters my home without my prior knowledge,' Vito replied smoothly.

Beneath his resting hands her stomach gave a quiver of dismay as a brand-new suspicion began to form like a monster, and she spun around angrily. 'This is all your doing,' she accused him. 'You told Marietta about Marcus and me. You helped her to arrange this!'

He didn't answer, and his expression was so coldly implacable that for Catherine it was an answer in itself.

Contempt turned her green eyes grey. 'I despise you,' she breathed, and turned back to look at the trio by the doorway just in time to see Marcus excuse himself to Luisa so he could come striding purposefully towards them.

He looked angry, he looked tense, and his eyes were filled with a mute plea for understanding even before he spoke. 'Catherine...' he said as he reached them. 'My sincere apologies, but I had no idea whose party this was until I was introduced to your mother-in-law just now.'

'It is called being set up,' Vito dryly inserted.

As Marcus glanced warily at him, Catherine took her moment to break free from his grasp and stepped towards Marcus. 'Dance with me,' she said, and before he could protest she had pulled him into the middle of the dance floor and placed herself firmly in his arms.

'I don't think your husband is pleased that we are doing this,' Marcus said uneasily.

Well, I'm not pleased with him, Catherine countered silently. 'Just smile, for goodness' sake,' she told him. 'And tell me what you are doing here.'

On a low groan that was packed full of contempt for his own gullibility, he explained about Marietta turning up at his offices that week, asking specifically for him. 'Having never heard of a Signora Savino before, I had no idea at all about her connection to the Giordani family.'

'She is my mother-in-law's goddaughter,' Catherine informed him.

'So I've just discovered.' Marcus nodded. 'She seems a nice lady, your mother-in-law,'

'She is,' Catherine confirmed. Shame about the rest of her family.

'But the goddaughter doesn't seem quite so nice.'

Catherine's eyes turned arctic grey. 'How did she get you here?' She prompted him to continue.

'With that magical word *business*,' he replied. 'And can we go somewhere less public, do you think?' he pleaded. 'Only I am beginning to feel distinctly *de trop* here...'

'Sure,' Catherine agreed, and stopped dancing to lead the way out through the open French doors which led into the lantern-lit garden, without even bothering to check out what Vito was doing. She wasn't interested. In fact, she didn't care at this moment if she never set eyes on the manipulative, vengeful swine ever again!

The air out here was warm and silken on the flesh. Catherine breathed in a couple of deep breaths of it, then said, 'Let's walk,' and began strolling down one of the pathways with Marcus pacing grimly beside her. 'Go on with your story,' she instructed.

'She lured me to Naples on the information that a well-known investment bank was looking for a new legal firm that specialises in European law,' he explained. 'When I asked her the name of the company she said she wasn't at liberty to give it until she had the go-ahead to make an official approach, but invited me over here this weekend—to meet some people—was the way she baited it. She sounded very plausible,' he added in his own defence. 'Extremely knowledgeable about what kind of legal expertise is required in the investment field.'

'She is,' Catherine confirmed. 'She owns stock in Giordani's, has a place on the board, holds some of their most lucrative portfolios.'

'Then she wasn't lying.' He frowned thoughtfully.

'About Girodani's wanting to change lawyers? I don't know, is the honest answer,' she replied. 'All I do know is that Marietta was one of the main causes for my marriage break-up three years ago. And since I came back here I have been expecting her to try the same thing again.'

'She's in love with your husband,' Marcus assumed from that.

Catherine didn't deny it, though she would probably use the word 'obsessed' instead of love. 'They work very closely together,' she murmured. 'Marietta is a natural charmer and Vito is—'

'Renowned for his troubleshooting qualities.' Marcus nodded. 'He turned Stamford Amalgamates round from bankruptcy in weeks only last year.'

'I didn't know that!' Catherine admitted, impressed without wanting to be, since most people knew that Stamford Amalgamates was about as big as a giant conglomerate could get.

'The fact that they were in trouble was kept secret to save the stock price,' Marcus explained. 'It was only after your husband had been in and waved his magic wand that those in the know discovered just how close things had been to collapse. He impresses me,' he added. 'Even though I don't want him to.'

'I know the feeling,' Catherine said grimly.

'Which means he's a dangerous man to cross.'

'I know that too.' She nodded.

'So why is Marietta attempting to cross him?'

'Because she is one of the only people Vito lets get away with it.' Catherine's smile was bitter.

'And the reason he does that?'

'Now there is the big question,' she mocked. 'I can give you a dozen maybes, Marcus. But no absolute certainties.'

'Okay,' he said. ' So give me the maybes.'

He was frowning thoughtfully—thinking on his feet just like Vito, Catherine likened wryly.

Which was probably why she liked him so much, she then realised, and didn't like the feel of that, since it also probably meant that she had always been looking for Vito-type qualities in every man she had come into contact with over the last three years.

'Because she is his mother's beloved goddaughter?' she suggested. 'Or because she was married to his best friend? Or maybe it could have something to do with the fact they are lovers?'

'Lovers in the past tense or the present?' Marcus asked sharply.

Catherine shrugged a slender shoulder. 'Both,' she replied.

'Rubbish,' Marcus denounced. 'That man has too much *nous* to play around with another woman when he's got you to come home to.'

Turning towards him, Catherine let her eyes soften. 'That was sweet of you,' she murmured softly.

But Marcus gave an impatient shake of his head. 'I wasn't being sweet, I was being truthful. I know men, Catherine. I am one myself, after all, so I should do. And I am telling you as a man that your husband is married to the only woman he wants to share his body with.'

Catherine stopped walking to turn sombre eyes on him. 'Then you tell me why you think you were brought here tonight?' she prompted gently.

He frowned, not understanding the question. 'It was Signora Savino who brought me here, in her quest to stir up trouble between you and your husband,' he replied.

'But who gave her the idea to use you as a weapon?' she posed. 'Who, in other words, told Marietta that you and I were more intimately involved than mere employer and employee?' she asked. 'Was it you who told her?'

'No!' he denied.

'And it wasn't me,' she said. 'Which leaves only one other person who knew about us.'

'Your husband?' Marcus stared at her in complete disbelief. 'You think your husband confided in that bitch about you and me?'

'Vito knew you were coming here tonight.' Catherine shrugged. 'He told me himself.'

'Then none of this makes any sense.' Marcus was frowning again. 'Because I can't see what either of them aimed to gain by bringing me face to face with you again. It served no useful purpose except to give us both a couple of embarrassing moments.'

He was right, and it hadn't. And they fell into a puzzled silence as their feet set them moving again—only to come to an immediate stop when the angry sounds of a familiar voice suddenly ripped through the air.

'You think you are so very clever, Marietta,' Vito rasped out. 'But what the hell do you think you have gained by bringing him here with you tonight?'

'Vengeance,' Marietta replied, and Catherine turned in time to see the metallic flash of Marietta's dress as it caught the light from one of the many hidden halogens. They were standing facing up to each other on the path that ran parallel with the one Catherine and Marcus were walking along. A neat boxed hedge surrounding a bed of pink roses was separating them. But that didn't mean Catherine couldn't see the malice in Marietta's face when she tagged on contemptuously, 'You have been flaunting Catherine at me since the day you married her—why the hell should I not flaunt her lover at you?'

'They were never lovers,' Vito denied as, beside Catherine, Marcus released a protesting gasp.

'They were lovers,' Marietta insisted. 'The same as *we* were once lovers! And when she tells you otherwise you know she is lying, Vito,' she added slyly. 'In the same way that she knows you lie every time you deny ever making love to me!'

'No,' Catherine murmured, closing her eyes as she waited tensely for Vito to deny the charge—now—when she could then let herself believe him at last!

But he didn't. 'That was a long time ago,' he bit out dismissively. 'Before I ever met Catherine—and therefore has no place in our lives today.'

Catherine felt Marcus's arm come around her shoulders when she must have swayed dizzily.

'It does to me!' Marietta insisted. 'Because you loved me then, Vito! You were supposed to have married me! Everyone expected it. *I* expected it! But what did you do?' she said bitterly. 'You settled for a short affair with me, then dropped me. And I had to settle for second best and marry Rocco—'

'Rocco was not second best, Marietta,' Vito denied. 'And he loved you—genuinely loved you! Which from the sound of it was more than you deserved from him!'

'Is that why you did it?' she asked curiously. 'Because Rocco loved me, did you step gallantly to one side and let him have me?'

'No. I stepped gallantly to one side because *I* didn't want you.' Vito stated it brutally.

'Shame you didn't let Rocco know that,' Marietta threw back. 'For he died believing he had come between the two of us.'

'Oh, my God.' Catherine breathed out painfully, remembering that bright shining star that had always been Rocco, scintillating the world while inside he must have been feeling wretched.

As wretched as she was feeling right now, she likened bleakly.

'When you brought Catherine here and made her your wife he actually apologised to me,' Marietta told Vito.

'Not on my behalf,' Vito rejected. 'Rocco knew exactly how I felt about Catherine.'

'Are you suggesting that you married her for love?' Marietta mocked. 'Don't take me for a fool, Vito,' she scoffed. 'Like everyone else around here, we all know you married her because you had to if you wanted to uphold family tradition and make Santo legitimate. If I had known that getting pregnant was what it would have taken to get you to marry me I would have used the tactic myself! But such a sneaky manipulation didn't occur to me—unlike her,' she added witheringly. 'With her cool English ways and clever independent streak that kept you dancing on your toes in sheer fear that she was going to do something stupid enough to risk your precious son and heir!'

'I think you've said enough,' Vito gritted.

'No, I haven't,' Marietta denied. 'In fact I haven't even got started,' she pronounced. 'You had the arrogance to think that all you needed to do was banish me to Paris and all your marital problems would be over. Well, they will never be over while I still have a brain in my head to thwart you with!'

'So you intend to do—what?' Vito challenged. 'Lurk in some more dark corners listening in on private conversations in the hopes that you can discover some more dirt to throw?'

'Ah,' Marietta drawled. 'So you knew I was there.'

'On the balcony next to ours? Yes,' Vito confirmed, unwittingly answering one question that had been burning a hole in Catherine's brain. 'When you later began quizzing Catherine about Marcus Templeton, I then found it a simple step to put two and two together and realise that you were planning to do something as—crass as this. But what I still don't understand is what you aim to gain by it?'

'That is quite simple. I mean to bring about the absolute ruin of your precious marriage,' Marietta coolly informed him.

'By bringing Marcus Templeton here?' It was Vito's turn to scoff. 'Do you really think that my feelings for Catherine are so fickle that I would throw her out because you brought me face to face with her supposed ex-lover?'

'No. But by having him here Catherine will have someone to fall upon when I tell her that I am pregnant with your baby.'

'That's a filthy lie!' Vito raked out harshly as Catherine swayed in the curve of Marcus's arm.

'But Catherine doesn't know that,' Marietta pointed out. 'She believes we have been lovers since before she lost your second baby. For a woman like Catherine, who cannot have more children, believing that I am pregnant with your child will finish her, believe me,' she advised. 'And I am going to enjoy watching her walk away from you with her darling Marcus after I break the news to her.'

'But why should you want to hurt her like that?' Vito demanded hoarsely.

'I couldn't care less about Catherine's feelings,' Marietta stated carelessly. 'But I do care about hurting you, Vito,' she told him. 'Just as you made me hurt when you passed me on to Rocco like a piece of used baggage!'

'You were lucky to have him!' Vito rasped out painfully. 'He was a good man! A caring man!'

'But not a Giordani.'

'My God,' Vito breathed, sounding truly shaken. 'Catherine was right. You are poison to whatever you come into contact with.'

'And, being so, I really do think, Marietta, that it is time for you to leave now.' Another voice arrived through the darkness.

Four people started in surprise, then watched with varying expressions as Luisa moved out from the shadows of yet another pathway. And the moment that she could see her face clearly Catherine felt her heart sink in sorrow. She looked so dreadfully—painfully wounded.

Yet what did Luisa do? She looked towards Catherine and murmured anxiously, 'Catherine, are you all right, darling? I would have given anything for you not to have witnessed this.'

It was almost worth having her cover exposed just to see the look of stark, staring dismay that was Marietta's face when she spun round to face her. But if it hadn't been for Marcus's arm grimly supporting her, she knew she wouldn't still be standing on her own feet, right now.

'Catherine—you heard...' Vito murmured, and sounded so relieved that it was almost painful.

'Well, well,' Marietta drawled. 'None of us are above lurking in dark corners to eavesdrop, it seems.'

But they were the satirical words of a woman who knew she was staring right into the face of her own ruin...

CHAPTER TEN

CATHERINE stood on the balcony watching the red tail-lights from the final few stragglers snake stealthily down the hillside.

The party was well and truly over at last, though it had gone on for another few nerve-stretching hours after Marietta had left here.

Marcus had taken on the responsibility of her removal, and the way he had guided her away without uttering a single word in anger to her Catherine had, in a strange way, found vaguely comforting. Because she was not the kind of person that liked to watch someone being kicked when they were already down, and Marietta had certainly been right down by the time that she had left.

It had been Luisa's icy contempt that had finally demolished her. Luisa who could usually be relied upon to find some good somewhere in any situation. But for once she had chosen not to, and watching a relationship that was as old as Marietta herself wither and die, as it had done out there in the garden, had been terrible.

Luisa had wept a little, which had helped to fill in an awkward moment between Catherine and Vito while they attempted to comfort her. And then there had been a house full of guests to sparkle for, plus questions to field about Marietta's whereabouts and...

She released a small sigh that sounded too weary for words, because she knew that this wretched night was still far from over.

'Quite an evening, hmm?' a deep voice murmured lightly behind her.

Too light, Catherine noted. Light enough for the true tension to come seeping through it. Vito knew as well as she did that, no matter what had been cleared up during that ugly scene in his garden, the two of them had not even got started yet.

'How is your mother?' she asked, without bothering to turn and look at him.

'She is still upset, naturally,' he replied. 'But you know what she is like,' he added heavily. 'She never could cope well with discord.'

'She loved Marietta.' Catherine stated it quietly. 'Discovering that someone you love is not the person you thought they were can be shattering.'

There was a moment of stillness behind her, then, 'Was that a veiled prod at me?' Vito asked.

Was it? Catherine asked herself. And shrugged her creamy shoulders because, yes, it had been a prod at him. 'You lied to me,' she said. 'About your previous relationship with Marietta.'

His answering sigh was heavy. 'Yes,' he finally admitted. And as that little truth came right out into the open he walked forwards, to come and lean against the rail beside her. 'But it happened a long time ago, and—arrogant as I am,' he acknowledged wryly, 'I did not think you had any right questioning me about my life before you came into it.'

'It gave Marietta power,' Catherine explained. 'With you persistently denying you'd ever been her lover, it left her free to drop nasty hints all over the place. When you insisted you were doing one thing she insisted you were doing another. And she...' Turning to look at him, she felt her soft mouth give a telling little quiver. 'She—knew things about you that only a lover would know.'

Wincing at the implication, he reached out to touch a

gentle fingertip to that telling little quiver. 'I'm sorry,' he said huskily.

It didn't seem enough somehow. And Catherine turned away from him to stare bleakly out across a now dark and very silent garden while beside her Vito did the same thing, their minds in tune to the heaviness Marietta had left behind her.

'She was out here that night, sitting on the next balcony listening to us bash out the same old arguments that we always used to share,' Vito said eventually. 'She must have lapped it all up. My continued lying, our lack of trust in each other, the mention of Marcus that must have seemed like a heaven-sent gift to her to use as yet another weapon.'

Standing in more or less the same place they had been standing that night, Catherine felt her skin begin to crawl at the mere prospect of anyone—worst of all Marietta— sitting there on the next balcony, eavesdropping on what should have been a very private conversation.

'How did you know she was there?' Catherine murmured.

'After you had gone back inside I remained out here, if you remember,' Vito explained. 'I was thinking—trying to come to terms with the very unpalatable fact that if your version of what happened the day you lost the baby was true, then a lot of other things you had said to me could also be true,' he admitted grimacingly. 'At which point I heard a movement on the next balcony—a chair scraping over the tiles, then a sigh I recognised, followed by the waft of a very distinctive perfume. Then I heard her murmur *"Grazie Caterina,"* and the way she said it made my blood run cold.'

He even shuddered. So did Catherine. Then, on a sigh that hissed almost painfully from him, he hit the stone balustrade with a clenched fist. 'How can you *know* someone

as well as you think you know them—yet not really know
them at all?' he thrust out tragically.

'She loved you.' To Catherine it seemed to explain everything.

But not for Vito. 'That is not love, it is sick obsession,'
he denounced. And his golden eyes flashed and his grim
mouth hardened. 'I decided she was out of my house by
the morning and I didn't care what it took to achieve it,'
he went on. 'So I went in to the office, worked all night
clearing *her* desk, not my desk, and the rest you know—
except that I used that week in Paris with her to let her
know that her place in this family was over.'

'What did she say to that?' Catherine asked curiously.

'She reminded me that my mother may not like to hear
me say that,' he dryly responded. 'So I countered that piece
of blatant blackmail—by sacking her from the bank.'

Catherine stared at him in stunned disbelief. 'Can you
do that?' she gasped.

His answering smile wasn't pleasant. 'She may own a
good-size block of stock in the bank, but not enough to
sway the seat of power there. And, although this is going
to confirm your opinion about my conceit, I am the main
force that drives Giordani's. If I say she is out, then the
board will support me.'

'But what about her client list—won't you lose a lot of
very lucrative business?'

'Given the option between going elsewhere with their
investment portfolios or transferring them to me, her client
list, to the last one, transferred to me,' Vito smoothly informed her.

'No wonder she was out for revenge tonight,' Catherine
breathed, feeling rather stunned by the depths of his ruth-
lessness. 'You frighten me sometimes,' she told him shakily.

Catching hold of her shoulders, he turned her to face

him. 'And you frighten me,' he returned very gently. 'Why else do you think we fight so much?'

Because I love you and I still daren't tell you, Catherine silently answered the question. 'We married for all the wrong reasons,' she said instead. 'You resented my presence in your life and I resented being there.'

'That is not entirely true, Catherine,' he argued. 'At the time I truly believed we were marrying because we could not bear to be apart from one another. '

'The sex has always been good.' She nodded.

His fingers tightened. 'Don't be flippant,' he scolded. 'You know we have always had much more than that.'

Did she? Catherine smiled a wry smile that made his eyes flash with anger.

'Is it too much to ask of you to give an inch?' he rasped out. 'Just a single small inch and I promise you I will repay you with a whole mile!'

'Meaning what?' she demanded, stiffening defensively in his grasp.

A nerve began to tick along his jaw. 'Meaning I married you because I was, and still am, head over heels in love with you,' he raked out. 'Will that help you to respond in kind?'

'Don't,' she protested, trying to turn away from him, knowing it wasn't true. 'You don't have to say things like that to make me stay here. Marietta didn't do that kind of damage.'

'It is the truth!' he insisted. 'And it should have been said a long time ago—I know that,' he admitted tightly. 'But now it has been said you could at least do me the honour of believing me!'

Staring up into those swirling dark gold burning eyes of his, Catherine wished—*wished* she dared let herself do just that. But...

Lifting her shoulders in a helplessly vulnerable gesture,

she murmured dully, 'A man in love doesn't go from the arms of a woman he loves straight into the arms of another.'

He went white in instant understanding, and she felt like crying for bringing it all up again. But it had to be said. It had to be dealt with.

His heavy sigh as he dropped his hands away from her seemed to be acknowledging that.

'I did *not* sleep with Marietta on the night you lost our baby,' he denied. 'Though after tonight's little revelations I can understand why you may choose not to believe that.' Glancing at her, Vito searched her face for a hint of softening, only to grimace when he didn't find it. 'You used to drive me crazy,' he confessed. 'From day one of our marriage you made sure I knew that you were not so content with your lot as my wife. You were stubborn, fiercely protective of your independence and so bloody steadfast in your refusal to let me feel needed by you—except in our bed, of course.'

'I needed you,' she whispered.

He didn't seem to hear her. 'As hot as Vesuveus in it and as cold as Everest out of it.' He sighed. 'I began to feel like a damned gigolo, useful to you for only one purpose...'

And I felt like your sex slave. Catherine silently made the bleak comparison.

'But at least I *could* reach you there,' he went on heavily. 'So I didn't take it kindly when you fell pregnant once again and were so sick with it that the doctors were insisting on no exertion—and suddenly I found myself robbed of my only excuse to be close to you when making love was banned also.'

'We made love!' she protested.

His eyes flashed darkly over her. 'Not the grit your teeth, feel the burn, all-out physical love we had always indulged in.'

'Life can't always be perfect, Vito!' she cried, shifting uncomfortably at his oh, so accurate description of their love-life.

'The sex between us was perfect,' he responded. 'We blended like two halves coming together in the fiery furnace. And I missed it when I wasn't allowed to merge like that any more, and I found the—other stuff,' he described it with a contemptuous flick of his hand, 'bloody frustrating, if you want to know.'

Listening to him so accurately describe how she had been feeling herself, Catherine stared at his grim face and wondered how two people could be so wonderfully in tune with each other—and yet not know it!

'So I grew more frustrated and resentful of what you did to me week by wretched week,' he went on. 'Until it all exploded in one huge row, followed by the most glorious coming together.'

'Then you stormed off.' She nodded, bringing this whole thing painfully back to where it had started. 'To Marietta, in search of consolation.'

'I stormed off feeling sick with my lack of self-control,' he brusquely corrected. 'But I did not start out at Marietta's apartment. I started out at the office—where she found me too drunk to do much more than let her take me home with her while I attempted to sober up before coming back to make my peace with you. Only it didn't work out like that,' he sighed. 'Because I fell into a drunken stupor on her sofa, muttering your name and pleading for your forgiveness. And the next thing I know I wake up, too many hours later to even count, to find myself in hell, where everything I held dear in my life was being wrenched away from me. By the time I stopped spinning round like a mad dog trying to catch its own tail, months later, I realised that I deserved what I had got from you—which only made me resent you all the more.'

'I felt the same,' Catherine confessed.

'But never, since the day I set eyes on you, have I so much as *wanted* to sleep with another woman—and that includes Marietta!' he vowed. 'In fact,' he then added reluctantly, 'the three years without you were the most miserable of my life, if you want to know the truth.'

Catherine smiled in wry understanding, and felt herself beginning to let herself believe him. Maybe he saw it, because he reached out to gently touch her cheek. 'But I never knew just how miserable until the night I picked up the phone and heard your voice...' he told her softly. 'It was as if someone threw a switch inside me to light me up.' He smiled.

'You were as cold as ice with me!' she charged.

'Not beneath the surface,' he denied. 'Beneath the ice I felt very hot and very angry—it was marvellous! Even fighting with you was wonderful,' he confessed as the hand moved to her throat, while the other slid stealthily around her waist to draw her up against him.

She didn't fight—didn't want to fight. She was too busy loving what he was saying here, with his eyes so dark and intense and so beautifully sincere.

'I was not in your home for five short minutes before I knew without a doubt that I was going to get you back in my life, no matter what it took to do it.' He stated it huskily. 'Because I want you here. I want you to *know* I want you here. I want to wake up every morning to see your face on the pillow beside me and I want to go to sleep every night with you cradled in my arms.'

Bending his head, he brushed his mouth against her own. 'In short, I want us to be a warm, close, loving family,' he said as he drew away again. 'Just me, you, Santo and Mamma, in a small tight unit of four with no lies to cloud our horizon and no— What?' he said, cutting off to frown at her as Catherine's softened expression took on such a radical change that he couldn't miss it. 'What did I just say? Why are you looking like that?'

She was already trying to get away from him. 'I...'

'Don't you dare claim that you don't want these things also!' he exploded angrily, completely misreading the reason for the sudden way she had just shut him out again. 'Because I know that you do! I *know* you love me, Catherine!' he insisted forcefully. 'As much as I love you!'

Oh, God help me! she prayed as his angry declaration shuddered through her. 'Please, Vito!' she begged. 'Don't be angry. But—'

'But nothing!' he growled, and took ruthless possession of her mouth in a blatant act meant to stop her from speaking.

It was hard and it was urgent, and she loved him for it. But in all her life Catherine had never felt so wickedly wretched—because he was trembling—all of him! His mouth where it crushed her mouth, his arms where they bound her tightly to him. She could even feel his heart trembling where her hand lay trapped against the wall of his chest.

And if she had never believed a single word he had said to her before this moment, then she suddenly knew that she had to believe that any man who could be as affected as this must truly love her!

'Y-You don't understand,' she groaned as she wrenched her mouth free of him. 'I need to—'

'I have no *wish* to understand,' was his arrogant reply. But it was hoarsely said, and the look on his face was the one Luisa would call his frightened expression. 'You are mine! You *know* you are!' And on that he picked her up and began striding inside with the grim-faced, hard-eyed, burning intention of ravishing her—Catherine knew that.

'You just said that you wanted no more lies between us!' She tried to plead with him for reason. 'Well, at least give me a chance to be as honest with you as you have just been with me!'

'No.' The refusal was blunt and uncompromising as he fell with her onto the bed.

'I do love you!' she cried—and effectively brought him to a stop just as his mouth was about to take hers prisoner.

'Say that again,' he commanded.

'I love you,' she responded obediently. 'But I have a terrible confession to make, Vito!' she hurried on anxiously. 'And I need you to listen before you—'

'If you are going to admit that you and Marcus Templeton were lovers,' he cut in, 'then believe me, Catherine, when I tell you that I do not want to hear it!'

'Marcus and I were never lovers,' she shakily assured him.

His eyes drew shut, long dark lashes curling over dark golden iris in an effort to hide his deep sense of relief. And Catherine's teeth pressed deep indentations into her lower lip as she waited while some of the fierce tension began to ease out of him.

She watched those eyelids rise up again slowly to show her the eyes of a man who was not quite as driven by fear any more, though still dark and dynamic, with the kind of inherent passions that curled around the soul.

'Okay,' he invited grimly. 'Make your damned confession and get it over with.'

'I *do* love you,' she repeated urgently. 'I always have! Wh-which—which is why I just couldn't do it!'

'Do what?' he frowned.

She lost courage, and with it the words to speak. So instead she kissed him gently, softly, tenderly. But her heart was beating like a hammer drill and, lying on top of her as he was, Vito had to be aware of it.

His head came up. 'For goodness' sake,' he breathed. 'It cannot be this bad, surely?'

The fear was filtering back into his eyes. She bit her bottom lip again. Then the tears began to flood her own eyes as she forced herself to say what had to be said.

'I didn't take the morning-after pills,' she confessed in a frightened little rush of words that had him staring down at her uncomprehendingly. 'I couldn't, you see, wh-when it came right down to it. I mean—how could I destroy the chance of a new life we may make between us? It was just too—'

'No,' he cut in as understanding finally began to dawn on him. 'You would not be so stupid.'

'I'm sorry,' she breathed. With trembling fingers Catherine reached up to gently cover the sudden white-ringed tension circling his mouth. 'But I couldn't do it. I just—couldn't do it...'

Rolling away from her, Vito jack-knifed to his feet, then just stood staring down at her as if he didn't know who she was. It was awful—much, much worse than she had expected it to be.

'What is it with you?' he demanded hoarsely. 'Do you harbour some kind of death-wish or something?'

Catherine sat up to hug her knees and murmured shakily, 'It was too late.'

He let out a laugh—only it wasn't a laugh but more a burst of something else entirely. 'No, it damn well wasn't!' he exploded. 'You had seventy-two hours to take the bloody things after we made love that day!'

'I meant it was too late for me!' she yelled back in pained rebuttal. 'What if we'd conceived, Vito?' She begged for understanding. 'It would have been like killing Santino!'

'That's just so much rot, Catherine, and you know it,' he denounced. 'You have been taking the contraceptive pill for years! What difference could a couple of extra hours be to what you do every single day?'

'Not then.' She shrugged. 'But the night before, when we...'

She didn't finish, but then she didn't need to. Vito was well ahead of her. 'That is no excuse,' he denounced, 'for putting your own life on the line!'

'We don't know if I have done yet,' she pointed out. 'But at least I can be sure that I didn't deliberately kill another baby.'

His face turned pure white. 'You didn't kill the last one!' he shouted furiously.

Catherine flinched at his anger. 'I don't want to talk about it,' she said, and buried her face in her knees.

'Well, you are going to talk about it!' he rasped, and a pair of hands gently took hold of her head to pull it upwards again. 'You are going to talk about the fact that once again you have made a decision that should have been mine to share with you!'

'You wanted me to take the pills!' she cried. 'That isn't sharing a decision; that's me bowing down to what you decide!'

'Well, that has to be better than this!' he said in a voice that shook, then removed his hands and turned right away from her.

'I'm sorry,' she whispered again, but he didn't acknowledge it. Instead he strode into the bathroom, slamming the door shut behind him.

And Catherine lowered her head again, allowing him the right to be so angry—which was why she had let him go on believing she had taken the damned—stupid—rotten pills!

And actually—she had meant to take them. It had only been when it had come to the point of actually putting them in her mouth that she'd discovered she just couldn't do it.

Not to herself, not to the child that might already have been forming its tenuous grasp for life deep inside her. So she'd binned the pills right there in Vito's bathroom then continued the lie with a determined blank disregard of the consequences.

Maybe Vito was right and she did harbour a secret death wish, she mused hollowly. But she knew deep down inside that this had nothing to do with death but to do with a chance of life. The maternal instinct to protect that life was as strong in a woman as the natural need to keep drawing in breath.

She hadn't been able to fight it, and somehow she had to make Vito understand that, she decided as she dragged herself off the bed and walked on shaking limbs towards the bathroom.

It had to mean something that he hadn't bothered to lock the door, she told herself bracingly as she twisted the handle and stepped bravely inside.

The room was steamy. Vito was already in the shower and his clothes lay in an angrily discarded heap over in one corner. Not really sure that she was doing the right thing here, Catherine walked over to the shower cubicle and pulled open the door.

He was standing with his back to the shower spray. Hands on narrow hips, wide shoulders braced, dark head thrown back to receive the full blast of the hot water right on his grim face.

A truly dynamic sensual animal, she mused, then smiled wryly at letting herself think of such things at a dire moment such as this.

'Vito,' she prompted quietly. 'We need to talk about this...'

His dark head tilted forward, then turned towards her. And his utterly cold dark golden eyes ran slowly over her while the water sluiced down his bronze back.

'You will ruin that dress in this steam,' was all he said, then turned his face back up to the shower.

Catherine gritted her teeth as her old enemy anger began to raise its dangerous head. And without thinking twice about it she stepped into the shower with him, silk dress and all, and firmly pulled the door shut.

She'd surprised him, she noted with some satisfaction as his dark head shot forwards again to stare at her in disbelief. 'What the hell do you think you are doing?' he protested.

'You are going to have to listen some time.' She shrugged determinedly. 'So it might as well be now.'

Forever the man to think fast on his feet, Vito responded by taking a small step sideways. Doing so gave the water spray unrestricted passage towards her, and, with a grim intention that galled, he leaned his shoulders into the corner of the shower, folded his arms across his impressive chest, then watched uncaringly as the water turned her red silk dress almost transparent before his ruthless eyes.

Diamonds glittered at her throat, at her ears, and on her finger. Her chin was up, her eyes flashing green fire at him at his black-hearted retaliation. But she didn't so much as gasp as the hot water hit her.

'Okay,' he said coolly. 'Talk.'

'I am a woman,' she announced, earning herself the mocking arch of an arrogant brow in response. Gritting her teeth, she ignored it. 'Being a woman, the urge to nurture and protect new life is so deeply entrenched in my very psyche that I would probably find it easier to shoot myself than harm that new life.'

'This is not the Dark Ages,' he grimly derided. 'In case you have forgotten, your sex stopped being slaves to your hormones a long time ago.'

'I'm not talking about hormones,' Catherine refuted. 'I am talking about instinct—the same kind of instinct that gives your sex the desire to impregnate mine!'

'Once again, *my* sex stopped being slaves to our sperm banks with the advent of condoms.' He also derided that.

'It is called free sex—enjoyed by millions for its pleasure, not its original function.'

'Since when have you ever thought of using a condom?' Catherine scoffed at that. 'I don't remember you considering protection, even when you knew it was dangerous for me to risk getting pregnant!'

His jaw clenched on a direct hit, and Catherine noted it with a nod in acknowledgement. 'You left the protecting up to me, Vito,' she reminded him. 'Which therefore gives me the right to call the shots when that protection is breached!'

'Not at the risk of your own life,' he denied.

'You said it,' she agreed. 'It *is* my life. I made a decision that might risk everything—but might also be risking absolutely nothing, depending on how my pregnancy goes. That's a fifty-fifty chance either way,' she told him. 'Fifty-fifty odds are just too even for me to justify stealing from any child the right to survive them!'

'For goodness' sake,' he rasped. 'Your own mother died in childbirth, Catherine! What does that tell you about the risk you are taking!'

Tears burst into her eyes, making them glint like the diamonds she was wearing. 'I didn't say I wasn't frightened,' she whispered shakily.

On the kind of curse that turned the air blue Vito snapped off the gushing water, then reached out to drag her against him.

'You stupid woman,' he condemned, but it was a darkly possessive and very needy condemnation. 'How could you do this to us now, when we are actually beginning to *know* each other?'

'I need you to be strong for me—not angry,' Catherine sobbed against his shoulder.

'I will be strong,' he promised gruffly. 'But not yet,

while I still cannot make up my mind whether I want to kill you for doing this to us!'

Despite the tears, Catherine lifted her face to smile wryly at him. 'That was a contradiction in terms if ever I heard one.'

He gave a muttered growl of frustration and bent to kiss her. Then, 'Turn around,' he commanded gruffly, and without waiting for her to comply he twisted her round himself, then began dealing with the sodden length of zip down one of her sides which helped hold the dress in place. With an efficiency that had always been his, he stripped her bare, and, leaving her clothes in a wet puddle on the shower floor, he led her out of the cubicle, found a towel and began drying her with all the grimness of a man still at war with himself.

Or with her, Catherine corrected as she gazed at the top of his dark head while he briskly dried her legs for her.

'It might never happen,' she huskily pointed out.

'With our past record?' His mouth took on a scornful grimace as he rose to his full height. 'You are pregnant, Catherine,' he announced as he wrapped the towel around her and neatly tucked the ends in between her breasts. 'You know it and I know it. We don't need to await the evidence to be that sure.'

'I'm sorry,' she murmured yet again, with a glum sense of utter inadequacy.

'But not regretful,' he said, clearly not very impressed by the apology.

Catherine gave a mute shake of her head. He reached for another towel, which he tucked around his own lean waist, then grabbed hold of her hand to lead her back into the bedroom.

The bed awaited. He trailed her directly to it, bent to toss back the covers—then paused. 'Your hair is wet,' he observed belatedly.

'Just the loose ends,' she dismissed, not in the least bit interested in her wet hair because she was too busy waiting for whatever it was he had damped down inside him to come bursting through the restraints of his control.

'I love you,' she said, and inadvertently helped it to explode when he turned on her, grabbed her by the shoulders and gave her an angry shake.

'You don't deserve me, Catherine,' he informed her darkly. 'You give me nothing but arguments, heartache and grief and yet I love you. You mistrust me, leave me, and make me go through the horror of fighting to see my own son, and still I continue to love you!'

'I didn't know that then,' she reminded him.

'Well, you damn well do now!' he grimly responded. 'So now what do I have?' he asked her. 'I have you back where you belong, is what I have. I have you back in my home, in my bed and in my life, and what do you do? You tell me I have to go through the worry and stress and fear of losing you all over again because you hold your own life in lower regard than I do.'

'It isn't that simple—'

'It is from where I stand,' he informed her. 'In fact it is elementary from where I stand! Because this time you are going to do as you are told. Do you understand me?'

His hands gave her another small shake. 'Yes,' she answered meekly.

'No more working for money we do not need. No more fights to establish your precious independence. You will rest when I tell you to, and eat when I tell you to, and sleep when I tell you to!'

'You're being very masterful,' she said.

'You think this is masterful?' he questioned darkly. 'Wait until you have lived for nine months with me as your jailer and you will be very intimate with just how masterful I am going to be!'

'Sounds exciting,' she said, her green eyes glinting up at him with the kind of suggestion that had him tensing.

'Well, that is just something else you are going to have to learn to do without,' he informed her deridingly. 'Because sex is out for the next nine months, if you recall.'

'Are you joking?' she flashed. 'I'm not giving up sex until I have to!'

'You will do as you are told,' he informed her coldly.

That's what you think, Catherine thought, with the light of battle burning in her eyes. On an act of rebellion she whipped both towels away, then, with a push to his arrogant chest, sent him toppling backwards onto the mattress.

'I want you now, while you are still wet from your shower and I am dripping in diamonds!' she informed him as she followed him down so she was stretched out down his full length. Then she kissed him so sensuously that he didn't stand a cat in hell's chance of arguing the point with her.

'You are right; you are a witch,' he muttered when she eventually released him.

'A happy witch, though,' she said. 'I love you. You love me. It makes me feel so wickedly aroused,' she confessed as she trailed the heart-shaped diamond locket across his kiss-warmed mouth. 'So, do you want to fight some more or make love?' she asked. 'Bearing in mind, of course, that you have just ordained that we are not allowed to fight any more...'

Eight months later, Catherine was relaxing on one of the sun loungers reading a book while Santo played around in the pool. It was April, and the weather had only just turned warm enough to indulge in this kind of lazy pastime. But she put her book aside when Vito suddenly appeared around the corner of the house and came to join her.

'You're home early,' she remarked, accepting his warm kiss as he bent over her.

'I have some news for you,' he explained. 'But first— how are my two precious females?'

Catherine smiled serenely as his hand reached out to lay a gentle stroke across her swollen stomach. Learning the sex of their baby had been a decision they had made together very early on in her pregnancy, when neither knew what the future was going to offer them. Catherine had wanted to know as much about her baby as she could know—just in case. And Vito had not demurred. So Abrianna Luisa had become a very real little person to all of them, and that included her brother and her grandmother. But in the end they needn't have worried, for she had sailed through this pregnancy without so much as a hiccup to spoil its calm, smooth development.

'We are fine,' she assured him. 'But—what is this?' She frowned as he dropped a very official-looking document with red seals and signatures on her lap.

'You can read Italian,' he reminded her lazily, then walked off to collect a red and white football that was lying beside the pool and toss it playfully at his son.

It was several minutes before he came back to her. By then Catherine had finished reading and was waiting for him. 'She sold out to you at last,' she said.

'Mmm,' was all he said, but his brief smile held a wealth of grim satisfaction. 'Once our daughter has arrived as safely as the doctors have assured us she will, I will have the stock transferred to her.'

'Not Santino?' Catherine queried.

Vito shook his dark head. 'He already has a similar block of my own stock placed in his name. So...' He bent down to touch a gentle hand to Catherine's stomach. 'Marietta's block will belong to my Abrianna Luisa,' he ordained. 'And we can now put Marietta out of our lives.'

With a sigh, Catherine gazed out in front of her and thought about Marietta, living in New York now and working for another investment bank of great repute. She was happier there, so they'd heard via the Neapolitan grapevine. Like any addict denied her fix, she had eventually learned to overcome her obsessive desire to be a Giordani. And, as Vito had just more or less said, her willingness to sell him her shares in the company was final proof of that. 'It's time Santo came out of the water before he catches a chill,' she murmured. And just like that Marietta was set aside.

Vito nodded. 'Santino!' he called. 'Come and help me heave Mamma off this lounger. It is time for her rest!'

'Rest,' Catherine mocked as she watched her son power his wiry little frame to the edge of the swimming pool. 'What else do I ever get to do but rest?'

'Ah,' Vito smiled. 'But this one will be different. For I shall be there to share it with you.'

And his eyes were gleaming, because he was talking about spending an hour or so loving her—not the sexual kind of loving, but the other kind, that nourished the soul…

HARLEQUIN *Presents*

Passion™

Looking for stories that **sizzle**?

Wanting a read that has a little extra **spice**?

Harlequin Presents® is thrilled to bring you romances that turn up the **heat!**

Every other month there'll be a
PRESENTS PASSION™
book by one of your favorite authors.

Don't miss
A MOST PASSIONATE REVENGE
by **Jacqueline Baird**

On sale October, Harlequin Presents® #2137

Pick up a **PRESENTS PASSION**™ novel—
where **seduction** is guaranteed!

Available wherever Harlequin books are sold.

HARLEQUIN®
Makes any time special ™

**Don't miss
an exciting opportunity
to save on the purchase of
Harlequin and Silhouette books!**

Buy any two Harlequin or
Silhouette books and save
$10.00 off future Harlequin
and Silhouette purchases

OR

buy any three
Harlequin or Silhouette books
and save **$20.00 off** future
Harlequin and Silhouette purchases.

*Watch for details
coming in October 2000!*

PHQ400

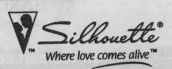

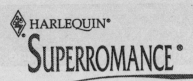

HARLEQUIN® SUPERROMANCE®

You are now entering

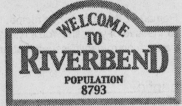

WELCOME TO RIVERBEND

POPULATION 8793

Riverbend…the kind of place where everyone knows your name—and your business. Riverbend…home of the River Rats—a group of small-town sons and daughters who've been friends since high school.

The Rats are all grown up now. Living their lives and learning that some days are good and some days aren't—and that you can get through anything as long as you have your friends.

Starting in July 2000, Harlequin Superromance brings you Riverbend—six books about the River Rats and the Midwest town they live in.

BIRTHRIGHT by Judith Arnold (July 2000)
THAT SUMMER THING by Pamela Bauer (August 2000)
HOMECOMING by Laura Abbot (September 2000)
LAST-MINUTE MARRIAGE by Marisa Carroll (October 2000)
A CHRISTMAS LEGACY by Kathryn Shay (November 2000)

Available wherever Harlequin books are sold.

HARLEQUIN®
Makes any time special ™

Visit us at www.eHarlequin.com

HSRIVER

Some secrets are better left buried...

Yesterday's Scandal by Gina WILKINS

A mysterious stranger has come to town...

Former cop Mac Cordero was going undercover one last time to
find and exact revenge on the man who fathered, then abandoned
him. All he knew was that the man's name was McBride—a name,
that is synonymous with scandal.

...and he wants her!

Responsible, reliable Sharon Henderson was drawn to the sexy-as-
sin stranger. She couldn't help falling for him hard and fast. Then
she discovered that their love was based on a lie....